DEADLY

ENCOUNTER

RYAN HODGE

SMP
PUBLISHING

SMP Publishing Edition

Printed in the United States of America

10 9 8 7 6 5 4 3 2 1

ISBN: 978-0-9977990-4-0 (PBK)

DEDICATION

To our mother:

So many precious moments we've shared,
your word and love were a protective blanket that
kept me from being scared.
The way we chilled, the way we hung out,
it wasn't about spending bread, it was about love, no
doubt.
You embodied what legends are made of,
your words of wisdom still guide me from your
position in the heavens above.
It's different without you down here rocking with us,
how could we not miss your unwavering love that was
simply gorgeous.
We were taught to never falter...never fail,
That's why in the absence of you in the tangible form,
we prevail.
Your love for us extended through every fiber of your
being,
and is still showering over us because your love was
true and never fleeing.

DEDICATION

"We Often Dream"

We often dream of many things,
we often wish for expensive clothes and diamond
rings.
We often dream of lavish trips,
and spending money carelessly like eating our favorite
chips.
We often dream of a big house and expensive car,
hoping one day to be a shining star.
We often dream of endless jubilation and fun,
only wanting to share special moments with that
special one.
We often dream to find the perfect one in which we
gel,
None of the things we dream, can compare to what
I've found in Mel.

CHAPTER 1

"Ooh! Ooh! Right there! Ooh, I'm bout to cum. Don't move, you are right on the spot! You're fucking this pussy so good right now!" I scream as I ride my husband's hard dick.

He always delivers it just the way I like it when it comes to sex. His name is Russell, but I call him Gem because he's a gem to me. He always treats me like the queen that I am. I'm not one to gloat, but he spoils me out of this world. I can honestly say that I'm one lucky woman. Gem buys me whatever I want, no matter how much it costs. It's almost like his sole purpose in life is to make me happy. I have so many pairs of designer shoes and handbags that I had to start giving them away.

Not only does he spoil me with material things, he also gives me plenty of affection. He opens doors for me, tells me he loves me, and totally respects me. I'm constantly a benefactor of back rubs, foot massages, and hot baths prepared for me accompanied by my favorite wine. Gem is really one of a kind and the best part about it is that he's all mine.

Oh, and I can't forget about the bedroom. Oh my, his sexual prowess is nothing like I've ever experienced before. The way he kisses me, fondles my body, and sexes me is something that most people only read about in books. Gem is always expanding our sex life. Every time I turn around, he has me in a new position and is seemingly pushing his dick further into my body. Gem is all man and has no shortcomings.

"Bounce on that dick! Yes, baby! Clap that ass on my shit," Gem orders as I ride his bull.

He slaps my ass sensually as I bounce and swirl on his dick. I'm turned on immensely from his grunts and ass slaps. I begin riding faster and bouncing off of his dick higher and higher, so I can feel every inch of his man stick. The mattress begins to slide off the bed as we fuck. Eventually, half of the mattress is hanging off the box spring and we fall to the floor. Gem's dick comes out of my soaked pussy just as I'm about to release my juices all over him.

We laugh as we hit the floor. Gem has sweat glistening on his brow and I wipe it away. He's always sexy, but there's something about him being sweaty and naked that drives me wild. Gem knows that I was about to cum when we fell off the bed. He motions me to sit on his face, so he can eat my pussy until I cum, but that's not how I want to orgasm right now. I want to feel his heavy dick in my stomach while it's banging on my walls.

"I want the dick!" I announce right before I begin licking the head of his cock.

Gem lets me suck his dick for a few minutes before he gives me what I want. His dick is harder than a steel beam. We get off the floor and lie back on the bed. Gem grabs me by my ass and pulls me close. We kiss passionately and he licks my neck. Just when I thought my sugar cave couldn't get any wetter, it does. Gem isn't even touching my pussy, but it's getting wetter and wetter every second we kiss. My juices are overflowing and I'm beyond turned on. My thighs are soaked from the juices escaping my peach.

"Gem, fuck me now! Please, baby. Stop teasing me. Don't do me like that. I want him now," I convey.

He rubs his dick between my legs and feels all the moisture down there. He grips his dick at its base and whacks my pussy with it. My eyes roll back in my head and I lick my lips. I reach down and play with my pussy and then stick those same fingers in Gem's mouth. He sucks the juices off of my fingers and then hoists me in the air and lies me on the bed. Gem climbs on top of me and inserts his pole of pleasure back inside of me.

He strokes me slowly. He strokes me fast. Gem strokes my pussy with his patented hula hoop maneuver. I start cumming all over his dick. While I'm cumming, Gem whispers in my ear.

"I love you. That was magical Kim. Better than ever. You were wonderful," Gem voices while kissing on my ear and neck.

I thank him and then kiss him back. Now, it's my turn to make him erupt. It's only right that I return the favor. I'm going to make his body quake just as he did mine. I may even get to cum again depending on how long we go for.

"How do you want me?" I ask as I lick his chest.

"Hmm, that's not so easy to answer because I want you all ways. I want you bent over, I want you in the car, and in the shower, and that's just to name a few. Let me think about it and then I'll be sure to let you give it to me the way I want," Gem articulates.

"Gem, stop playing. Hit it from the back. I know you like to fuck from the back and get you a thunderous nut," I speak.

I put my face down in the pillow, arch my back, and toot my ass in the air, just the way Gem likes it. I smack my ass to entice him, but Gem doesn't make a move. Instead, he gets off the bed and stands up. Oh, he wants to fuck me from the back while he stands at the edge of the bed. Gem doesn't like fucking from the back on his knees because he feels that's for amateurs. I immediately, slide to the edge of the bed and put my face down and ass up again. Gem still doesn't touch me.

"Honey, I'm gonna get ready for work. We'll finish what we started later tonight when I get home," Gem verbalizes.

"You didn't nut though. You can't go to work like that. I'm going to take care of that before you leave," I respond.

"It's okay, as long as you came. I just wanted to satisfy you. I'll be fine throughout the day. Besides, I'll have all day to think about how I'm gonna serve you this dick tonight. The anticipation is gonna drive me wild all day long. When I get my hands on you tonight, it's going to be the rumble in the jungle," Gem tells. "I don't always have to nut to be satisfied. As long as my queen is satisfied, I'm good."

I don't say anything further. Instead, I let Gem get in the shower, so he can go to work. See, that's why I love him so much. He's always selfless when it comes to me. My previous lovers were always chasing a nut and never really aimed to please me. It seemed like they were only about pleasing themselves. I knew there was something special about Gem from the first time we met. We met four years ago at In the Mix.

I was twenty-four at the time and was partying heavy and all about having a good time.

While, at In the Mix, I saw Gem at one of the tables. He immediately caught my eye because he was sharply dressed. I mean he was sharper than a Ginsu knife. He was like a movie star on the red carpet of an award show type of sharp. I wanted to meet him, so I staged a meeting, but I made it seem like it was accidental. With the help of Sage, Gem and I were talking in no time at his table.

Gem was a great conversationalist. He knew a little something about everything. I found myself being lost in is brown eyes that were marble-like. He stood at an even six feet tall and towered over me. I've always been drawn to men with wavy hair and a neatly trimmed goatee. Gem had exactly that. I knew this man was sent just for me. Gem had a muscular body, but wasn't too bulky. He was just perfect. After talking to him for a while and having a few drinks, I decided that I would have a one-night stand with him. I'll never forget that night.

"So, what are your plans for the night once you leave here?" Gem inquired.

"Well, I don't have any plans for the rest of the night or in the morning, so I guess I'll be going home," I answered.

Gem stated, "I feel you on that. I'm free myself. I don't have anything pertinent happening for tonight or tomorrow. I'm just gonna go home to chill."

"Oh, okay. That's surprising because I

figured that you'd have something lined up for tonight. It's still gonna be fairly early when we get out of here tonight," I said.

"Yeah, it will still be early, but I don't have anything planned," Gem replied.

"Well, if you're not doing anything and I'm not doing anything maybe we can link up afterwards. You can come to my place," I suggested as I flipped my hair to the side.

Gem took my suggestion well. He agreed to us linking after leaving the lounge. Gem suggested that we meet at a pancake house that he liked. I told him that he can just eat at my place and that I'd cook for him. Gem liked that idea even better than going to the pancake house. We were all set to link up later and I was elated because I knew I was going to get some dick. It had been far too long since the last time I had sex and my tut-tut was ready to be penetrated. I was so ready that I went a little overboard with my words that night. I immediately found out the type of man I was dealing with.

I spoke, "If you don't do anything to blow it for yourself, I might even let you get a taste of something other than my cooking."

"Is that right? What else do you have in mind for me to taste?" Gem asked.

I was feeling good and the few drinks I had were really talking to me. I was feeling myself and really needed some dick, so I was straightforward with him. I told Gem that he could taste me sexually if he was up to the challenge. However, I really didn't expect to get the answer I got from him.

"Kim, you're beautiful! I mean really, really beautiful! I will blow your back out if I give you this dick. I'm telling you that I'd have you walking funny for a few days. I know you may hear that a lot because all dudes brag about their shit, but I'm different. Sexually, I'm a juggernaut," Gem voiced confidently.

"I've heard that a thousand times before in my lifetime. I'd rather you be about it than to talk about it. You're probably a minute man, since you're speaking so highly about your sex game," I shot back.

Gem replied, "Nothing close to a minute man. In fact, many women haven't been able to make me climax. Honestly, whether or not my dick game is official or not really isn't even the real question. It starts before that."

"Well, what's wrong with you that women can't make you cum? Do you have limp dick syndrome? Where does it start if it doesn't start with it being official?" I asked

"Trust me. My dick is long, thick, and strong! I've never had anyone question my length, width, or stamina. Where the conversation starts is the fact that I don't want to have sex with you," Gem orated sternly.

I'm not going to lie and say that I wasn't taken aback. Really, I was crushed because I was too damn fly for him to say he didn't want to fuck me. I was looking damn near the best I've ever looked in my life and he told me that he didn't want me. Additionally, I was slightly embarrassed that he rejected me after I practically threw myself at him. That blue dress was hugging every inch of my tight frame. I'm five foot three and chocolate as can be. I have long and healthy flowing black hair that most women would love to have. Not to mention, my ass is juicy and soft as hell. Normally men are falling all over me, but not this man. Gem had to be gay if he wasn't interested in me. I had to find out.

"You can just tell me that you're gay. Cause it can't be anything else. All of the sexy brothers are gay these days," I stated.

"Hell no, I'm not gay! I'm totally heterosexual. I love beautiful brown sisters such as you," he said.

"Well, if you like women, you just said that I'm beautiful and your dick works, so I don't get why you don't want to fuck me," I verbalized.

"I know it seems complicated, but it's really not. Let me explain. It's not that I would never have sex with you because I would. As I said, you're beautiful and I'm sure any man would want to have sex with you, but I don't have sex just to get a nut. For me, sex means something. It's something that's pure... It's a connection between two people and once you have sex with someone, you two are forever connected. Since that's the case, I don't just run around fucking everything moving like I'm a college boy. Basically, when I have sex, I make love and I dedicate myself to fulfilling every erotic need my partner may have," Gem narrated.

I was at a loss for words when he explained himself. The drinks that had me slightly tipsy now had no impact on me. His sincere and frank words had a sobering effect on me. I felt like a little hoe for throwing myself at him after hearing how he regards sex. I was sure he'd have nothing to do with me after I exposed myself like that, but I was wrong. Gem didn't judge me. He even let me blame it on the alcohol. I definitely needed a scapegoat that night. We conversed further.

"Well, I apologize if I offended you. I should've never assumed that you wanted to have sex with me tonight," I said.

He spoke, "No, need to apologize. It's cool. It's not like we're little kids or something. We're grown and that's what grown people do."

"You're right, but I'm still sorry. It's just that most men are always chasing a nut, so I just figured you were like the others. It's wrong to assume that all men are the same," I chimed in.

"That's very true. We're not all the same. I'm the type of person to fortify a friendship first. During that friendship building, I hope to like her as a friend and then my feelings are formed. If I don't know a woman and genuinely like her, I can't have sex with her. It's just not in me to proceed that way. There's no way I'm going to pleasure a woman sexually and I barely know her. In my opinion, that would be a slap in the face to my future mate," Gem articulated.

"I understand. That's very special and that's how it should be. What you're saying is quite refreshing. I can honestly say that I've never heard that before. That's very noble and I commend you for that. A man who is in control of his dick is a rarity," I mentioned.

"Now, if you want to go get a one-night stand, I'm not the guy for you. There's still some time for you to get you someone to lay up with tonight. You're very attractive and that dress is really showing how well-endowed you are back there, so I'm sure it won't be hard. On the other hand, you can stay here chatting with me. I'm willing to forget about most of what we discussed tonight if you decide to stay," Gem worded.

I may have been a little hot in the pants back then, but I wasn't a fool. I could always tell a good man when I saw one and still can today. I decided not to seek a one night stand any further and chilled with Gem. I knew I couldn't pass him up.

"Boy please, I'm not worried about anyone other than you tonight. That one-night stand was motivated by all of those drinks I had, but I'm thinking clearly now. I'm totally over that," I declared.

Gem responded, "That's good to know,

so…"

Something Gem said moments before had clicked in my head. He stated that he'd forget most of what we discussed tonight. I've always been extremely nosy, so I had to inquire about what he was going to remember. It would have killed me if I didn't. I cut him off while he was in the middle of his sentence.

"Did you say that you were going to forget some of the stuff we discussed? Well, what do you plan on remembering?" I inquired feverishly.

Gem laughed as he answered, "I'm not forgetting that you said you were making breakfast. I'm still trying to get that, if you're up for it."

Gem and I left shortly after that and went to my house. I cooked us a late-night breakfast. We talked into the wee hours of the morning and then Gem left. That was our first encounter and I've never stopped respecting him since. Gem's a keeper and I'm not letting him go. He comforts me in ways I didn't even know I needed to be comforted. What a perfect blend of a man. He's strong, not overly sensitive, and always keeps his word. He told me that first night that he meets every erotic need that his woman has and he has definitely lived up to every letter of that statement. He's been feeding my mind, body, and soul ever since. We make beautiful music together no matter what we do. The craziest thing is that we seldom have disagreements.

I want to stay in the bed after the way Gem made me release, but I don't. Instead, I slowly ease out of the bed and head to the laundry room to iron Gem's work clothes. Gem's a best-selling author and is a professor at Howard University. Also, he goes around the country giving speeches and gets paid very well for them. I run the business side of Gem's company. I'm also in charge of all of his press events. Gem and I work very well together. Gem exits the bathroom after taking his shower and gets dressed.

"Thanks for ironing my clothes," Gem speaks.

"You're welcome. If you want breakfast, I can whip something up real quick," I offer.

"I'm fine on the breakfast. I'll grab something on campus if I get hungry. You just be ready to quench my appetite tonight when I get home. It's gonna be on," Gem voices as he grabs my ass tightly and gives me a peck on my lips.

Gem leaves for work and I clean up around the house. After I do that, I get showered and dressed. I have to go to the bookstore to set up a book signing for Gem. He's releasing a new book soon, so I have to get some things in place for once it hits the shelves.

CHAPTER 2

Tonight's a big night for Gem. Well, not just for Gem, it's a big night for the both of us. Gem's new book entitled "Earth is Dead" was released today and we're having a huge book release party for him tonight. The party is going to be at In the Mix and is going to be awesome. Gem is good friends with Sage McMillian, who is the owner of the venue. Also, today is Gem's birthday, so he's extra excited and is double dipping his celebration. The party tonight will serve as his book release party and birthday celebration all wrapped up into one.

I'm Gem's publicist, so all of the planning for tonight is on me. That's why it's a big night for me too. Everything has to be perfect. I don't like for my name to be attached to anything that isn't flawless. The great part about tonight is that the festivities aren't going to cost Gem and I a dime. Since I coupled Gem's birthday celebration with his book release party, Gem's publishing company is footing the bill. I love the way my conniving mind works sometimes. Hey, there's nothing wrong with a night of glamour especially when it's for free. Watch me work!

It's going to be a night of glamour for sure. Many of Gem's celebrity friends are attending the celebration tonight. The party is by invitation only, so there won't be any unruly people in the building. Sage was kind enough to close his venue to the public for the night just for Gem. I've invited many of Gem's classmates from his college days. I'm sure they'll show their support as they always do. It's going to look like Howard University's yard at In the Mix tonight and I know Gem's going to love it.

Hell, I can't even front like he's the only one who's going to enjoy it because I know I am too. On a normal night, In the Mix is the most popping lounge in D.C. and tonight is nothing close to normal, so I know the party atmosphere tonight will surpass all before it. I still have a few more things to get accomplished before this evening. There's always so much to do in so little time. I walk into the bathroom before I leave the house, so I can check myself over.

I gently brush my hair to fix the wild hairs and freshen up my makeup. I turn to the side and see how juicy my booty looks before I exit the bathroom. It looks delicious and now I'm ready to run my errands. My phone begins to ring as I'm walking out of the house. I know it's Gem calling to make sure everything is copasetic for tonight. He's a slight perfectionist when it comes to his work and when he's on public display, his need to be perfect is aggrandized one hundred percent. I pull my phone out of my bag and look at the screen. To my surprise, the caller isn't Gem; it's Sage. I wasn't expecting a call from Sage, so I immediately think that something is wrong. I feel a quick fit of panic in my stomach as I answer the phone.

"Hi, Sage," I say.

"Hi, I just wanted to reach out to you in regards to tonight," Sage voices.

"Thanks for reaching out to me. Is everything alright?" I inquire.

Sage answers promptly, "Oh yeah. Everything is fine. I just make it a habit of calling my clients the day of an event to make sure there isn't anything else they need of my staff and me."

"I guess I can stop holding my breath. I almost pissed my pants when I saw your number flashing on my screen. I just knew there was something wrong. Don't scare me like that. Next, time just send me a text, please," I verbalize.

Sage lets out a chuckle as he assures me that everything is fine. Also, he apologizes for scaring me like that. I accept his light-hearted apology. The conversation doesn't last much longer after I tell him that I don't have any last-minute needs for tonight. Sage is a very nice guy and is very professional. He reminds me of Gem in that fashion. I'm a proud graduate of Howard University and I'm even more proud that Howard University is graduating men of esteem like Gem and others. I pull away from my home to run my errands.

Hours pass and I'm almost done with all that I had to do. I only have two more stops to make. I have to go to the bakery to pick up the cake for tonight and drop it off at In the Mix. I could have had it delivered, but I need to control as many aspects of tonight as possible. I pull up to the bakery and go inside. The clerk greets me and gets my cake. I look it over and all is well with the cake, so I depart and drop it off at the lounge. I drive home and see Gem's car as I'm pulling up. I walk inside, but don't immediately see Gem. As I'm walking upstairs, I hear the shower running. I open the bathroom door and see my husband's silhouette in the shower. I walk over to the shower and fling the door open.

"Well, I'm glad you're okay! I called and texted you earlier," I speak.

Gem words, "My battery died, but I didn't know until I went to make a call. I picked up my phone and realized then that it was dead. I wasn't anywhere long enough to charge it. I was busy as hell! I apologize."

"It's cool. You know how my nerves get when

I don't hear from you for extended periods of time. My mind starts racing all over the place. You know D.C. isn't the safest place on earth. Between the way cops are killing black men and the way black men are murdering other black men, I'm always fearful," I orate.

"I hear you, but I'm fine. By the way, you're more like paranoid than fearful," Gem jokes.

I know that Gem is busy making calls and setting things up, so his phone is constantly being used. No need to cry over spilled milk. Gem and I converse as he finishes showering. I take my clothes off in preparation for my shower. As Gem steps out of the shower, I go to step in after him. While squeezing past him, he grabs me by my ass and pulls me to him. His grasp sends an erotic tingle through my body. I love when Gem grabs me with force. I'm getting slightly moist from his clutch.

"You gonna let me taste some of that?" Gem asks as he stares at me with his warm brown eyes.

I see lust and desire in his eyes. I know he wants to bend me over, right here and now in this bathroom as he's done masterfully on so many occasions. I envision him smacking my ass and his rod stretching the walls of my pussy and right when I think it can't get any better, I'll cum all over his dick.

"You want it right now? You want me to bend over and let you slow grind or pound my sweet hot pussy?" I inquire in a seductive tone.

"Baby, you know exactly what I like. I want you to do exactly that and more. Me bending you over will be like an appetizer to a full course meal," Gem answers.

I push away from him and bend over on the double vanity sink. I'm positioned right in front of the mirror. I look in the mirror and see his dick becoming fully erect. I smack my ass with one hand and suck my finger in a sexually enticing manner. Gem walks over to me and smacks his hard dick on my ass.

"I love when you smack your dick on my ass!" I state.

"I know you do and you're gonna love the way I stroke your coochie even more," Gem promises.

"I know that's true. I know what else you know too," I reply.

"Oh yeah? What else do I know?" Gem asks.

I respond, "I know that you know that ain't no way I'm letting you get none of this before I wash my body. I've been out all day long and I'm not fresh at all. You know I don't get down like that."

"Kim, you know you're wrong for that. Let me just put the head in for two seconds. I just want to feel her real quick," Gem remarks as he laughs.

I utter as I breeze past Gem and head for the shower, "Boy bye! I'm not following you up. You won't ever be able to say that I didn't smell good."

"I know how you feel about that. I get it… it's a woman thing. You know men don't care one bit. We'll have a full-blown fuck session right after playing three games of basketball. We won't even consider taking a shower," Gem voices.

"Oh, I know. That's cause y'all just nasty and always chasing a nut. Well, not you, but you're one in a billion. You're my Gem," I tell.

Gem laughs, but he knows I'm right. Now, I have a decision to make. I know that we won't have time for a sex session after I shower because I'll have to shower again afterwards. Like I said to him, there's no way that I'm making love to my husband knowing that my kitty isn't fresh as can be and my body may be slightly salty from perspiring out in the heat all day. I also know that I can't leave his dick hard and throbbing like it is, so what should I do? I do what any woman who has a loving and loyal man would do.

"I guess we're both special because you're my one and only," Gem comments.

Without saying another word, I walk over to Gem and kiss him on his chiseled chest. I pin him against the vanity, so he can't move. I stroke his long dick with both hands and drop down to my knees. Next, I order him to hold my hair. I lick his dick and start sucking it until he cums all over my titties. I jump up and beeline for the shower. A minute later, I peer out of the shower and notice Gem still hasn't moved.

I yell out, "Baby, are you okay?"

"Yes, I'm fine! I needed that release. Damn, I needed that! I'm still getting my bearings straight," Gem words.

"Oh, okay. I'm glad you enjoyed it. You damn sure nutted faster than normal. I'll let you have all of me tonight after the party," I say.

"All of you? You promise?" Gem wants to know.

"Yes, I promise. You can have whatever you want for your birthday!" I confirm.

"Baby, alright, but you better be ready. We'll call what you just did to me the appetizer. I hope you're going to be ready for the rest of dinner," Gem articulates.

"Honey, I'm always ready and tonight will be no different. I'll bet my last on that. Now stop bothering me and let me shower. You go and get dressed. You can't be late to your own party. That'll be bad for business," I vocalize.

"If we're late, it won't be because of me. I'll be dressed in no time. I'm always on time," Gem comments.

"Are you taking shots at me? Are you implying something about me?" I ask.

Gem doesn't answer my questions. Instead, he just exits the bathroom without saying anything. However, I know he was trying to be funny. I've been known to be late a time or two, but it's only because I always want to look beautiful for myself and my husband. I represent both of us when I step out, so I make sure that I'm never caught looking substandard. I finish my shower, dry off, and exit the bathroom. I get dressed and do my hair and makeup. I clean up nicely if I do say so myself. Gem and I are wearing matching colors tonight. I'm wearing a black dress with red accessories with a pair of black red bottoms. He's wearing a black suit with a red dress shirt and a black tie. We are suited and booted. Gem walks in as I'm giving myself one last look over.

"Man hasn't created a word, phrase, symbol, or language that can adequately express how gorgeous you are," Gem compliments.

"Aww, Gem! Thank you! That was so sweet. You're gonna make me tear up and ruin my makeup," I respond.

"No, thank you for holding me down. It means everything to me. I may not always say it, but you're my world!" Gem states as he swoops in and gives me three pecks on my lips.

"You're welcome Russell. You mean the world to me too," I say.

"I know and I also know that it's time to roll. Like you said, I can't be late to my own party. We have to be there to greet the first guest. It's only right because of the support they're showing us," Gem explains

"I couldn't agree more, so let's roll. I'm ready on time, this time," I offer as I pop my neck.

I grab my bag and Russell and I depart.

Gladly, we make it to In the Mix before any of the guests arrive. We walk inside and Sage greets us with his wife Sheena. We review the order of events for the night with Sage and then he conferences with his staff. Gem and I walk over to the door, so he can greet the guests and take pictures on the red carpet if they want one.

CHAPTER 3

Gem's party is going excellently. The party is flowing just as I envisioned it, every detail. There have been no hiccups with anything. The music is perfect for dancing and mingling. In the Mix is impeccably adorned and Sage's staff is not missing a beat. Gem's birthday party and book release party is a success. The evening is a success because everyone's enjoying themselves and Gem is extremely happy with the turnout. Everyone he invited to the event is here now. All of his Howard alumni buddies showed up and his friends from New Jersey and South Carolina are here too. Additionally, there are many guests here who work for magazine and newspaper companies. On top of that, Gem can't stop selling and autographing books. The support that people are showing is full throttle. I know Gem's new book is going to be another hit. Surprisingly, some people who bought the book tonight have already started reading it.

I don't see myself reading a book in a nightclub, but I'm not judging anyone. To each his own. The fact that people are willing to read a book while at a nightclub is evidence that Gem's work is phenomenal. I'm working the crowd and mingling with as many patrons as possible. I've sent countless people over to Gem's table to purchase a book. We're working the venue from both ends. Sage's idea to allow a limited number of regular In the Mix patrons into the lounge tonight turned out to be priceless.

It was a great idea because it gives Gem and his novels more exposure. Some people who were not aware of Gem's work are now in the know. Many of them have even gone to Gem's table to show support. It's always a good feeling when your people support you. Many of them are taking pictures with Gem and sharing them to their social media accounts. My phone begins to vibrate while I roam the lounge.

I take my phone out of my pocket to check it. I see that Gem has sent me a text asking me to bring him a bottle of water. He's been terribly busy and hasn't had a moment to step away and grab something to drink himself. I can see that the bar staff is extremely busy, so I can't blame them for not getting to him. I walk over to the bar to get Gem a bottle of water. While I'm waiting, I notice a woman staring at me. I thought we made eye contact earlier, but I didn't think too much of it, but now she's staring at me again. I don't know what to think. I'm sure I don't know her because I never forget a face.

The bartender is near me, so I get his attention and ask for a bottle of water. I thank the bartender and turn to walk over to Gem. When I turn around, the woman who was staring at me is right beside me. She is so close to me that I almost bump into her. I take a step back to get some distance between her and I.

"I'm sorry. I didn't mean to almost run you over. I should have been more attentive," I voice.

"No, no. I apologize. I should have given you your distance. I guess I'm a bit of a space invader," the unknown woman utters.

I speak jokingly, "Well, I guess we can call it a double fault."

"Yes, I would have to claim fault. Double fault works for me. If you want to claim culpability for me riding your shoulder, I'll let you do that," she replies.

"Truth is truth. I was at fault. I'm just glad I had a bottle of water instead of a drink because if I didn't, we'd both be covered in alcohol right now. Another thing, I think we made eye contact earlier this evening," I word.

"Girl, yes! We would be in the bathroom blotting our dresses right now. We may have even been mad enough to come to blows. I'm kidding about coming to blows and yes, we did make eye contact earlier," the woman replies.

"Chile, you know you are a mess, don't you? I didn't think I was crazy; do we know each other?" I inquire.

"I love joking around, but seriously, I apologize for almost colliding into you. No, we don't know each other, but I did want to make your acquaintance tonight. I tried to talk to your husband, but he hasn't had a minute to spare, so I wanted to meet you," she explains.

"Is that right? What can my husband and I assist you with?" I ask. "Do you think because you're gorgeous that my husband would want to talk to you?"

"I'm sorry! My manners are without me tonight. I'll blame it on the alcohol. My name is Cassie Monroe and I'm the CEO of *Black People Magazine*. My wanting to talk to your husband wasn't for anything underhanded. I would like to have your husband on the cover of my magazine. Since I couldn't talk to him, I asked Sage what I should do and he pointed me in your direction. I think it'd be great for both parties," she verbalizes.

"Oh, no need to apologize. It is one of those nights. I'm Kim Davenport. It's very nice to meet you. I love your magazine. I've been a subscriber for quite some time," I tell. "Russell would love to be on the cover of your magazine."

"Yes, it's definitely one of those nights. Nice

meeting you as well! Thank you for your patronage. It's good to know that you support black owned businesses. Honestly, I already knew that you had a subscription to the magazine. I had my assistant check through our subscriber's list and your name was on it. I know you're busy tonight, so I won't keep you any further. Here's my card. Call me next week and we'll set up a time for you and your husband to come in," Cassie Monroe orates.

I respond, "You must be very meticulous in what you do to know your subscribers by name…and as far as setting up a meeting, that's excellent! We'll be in touch next week for sure. Russell will be excited."

"I am very meticulous in what I do. I'm a borderline stalker when it's comes to finding out what I want to find out. You see I stalked you in here until I eventually bumped into you. Literally and figuratively," Cassie says humorously.

"You're hilarious. I can't with you… I can't. I feel you on being meticulous. Girl, I planned this party to the 'T'. I couldn't sleep some nights because I couldn't stop playing the night over and over again in my head. I have a knack for the fine details of situations," I recite.

"Yes, that's me all the way. Can't stop thinking about a task until it's complete. While it's going on, I'm a wreck and when it's done, I analyze what I could've done to make it better. I love planning things out. Well, you did a great job putting this together," Cassie verbalizes.

I agree with everything she says because that's how I always am. I second guess everything. Hell, I even triple guess it. Cassie and I converse for a while longer. I didn't want to end our conversation to take Gem his bottle of water, so I sent it over to him with one of the waitresses. Cassie is quite the conversationalist and doesn't ever stop talking. I don't mind one bit because she's cool, but more importantly, Cassie, can take Gem's career to another level. If giving her some of my time will help foster Gem's career, I'm all for it. I really want her to meet Gem tonight. It looks like Gem isn't busy like he was earlier, so we walk over to him.

"Gem, I want you to meet Cassie Monroe. She's the CEO of *Black People Magazine*," I introduce.

"Cassie, it's nice to meet you. I'm Russell Davenport. I love your magazine! We read them all the time. What you do for people of color is to be applauded. We appreciate you tremendously," Gem reports.

"Russell, thank you. The pleasure is all mine. I appreciate the role model you've been to our people. Your commitment to helping people who are less fortunate is to be commended," Cassie shoots back.

"Honey, Cassie wants you to appear on the cover of her magazine and potentially participate in some other endeavors going forward. I had to bring her over here to meet you," I voice.

"I'm all for it! Well, let me not speak too quickly. My wife is in charge of all of that type of stuff, so if she's on board, I am too. If she isn't with it, then I'm not either," Russell comments.

"Oooh, girl! You have this fine brother trained, I see. I knew I liked the way you operate. Black girls rock! Well, I'll be sure to communicate everything through your wife," Cassie remarks.

"Girl, damn right I do! It took a while, but I have him all trained up. It ain't nothing but Black Girl Magic!" I chime in jokingly.

"I see both of you are crazy as hell! I knew you were special when I noticed you commandeering my wife's time for so long. It would take a beautiful and successful woman to keep my wife from delivering me a bottle of water. You did what no man could ever do," Russell vocalizes humorously.

Cassie attempts to respond to Russell's comment, but as she utters a few words, his attention is taken by a fan of his who wants an autograph and picture. In the matter of seconds, Russell is jammed packed with followers at his table. Cassie and I leave him to handle his business. We find ourselves having drinks on the dance floor, partying, and laughing at people who look ridiculous while dancing. I'm glad I bumped into her because I needed this type of fun tonight. This is much better than stressing about every detail of the night. We leave the dance floor and have a bottle delivered to our VIP booth.

"I must say, you have it all," Cassie offers out of the blue.

"What's that?" I ask as I pour our drinks.

"The life! You have a successful husband who is handsome and seems to love you to death. That's the life. Not to mention, I know your sex life is amazing," Cassie answers.

"I can't lie and say that life isn't grand because it is. And as far as my sex life goes, good girls never tell," I communicate.

"Girl, I hear you. No need to tell because I've read Russell's books, so I know he's putting it down. You're lucky. Just know that," Cassie tells me as she sips her wine.

The truth is that I know that I'm lucky. Hell, Gem is lucky too. We both are lucky and our sex life is the bomb dot com. I'm a freak at heart and so is Gem. We communicate great and are in complete harmony most of the time. Russell's my guy and I'm his gal. We've been inseparable from day one. Cassie and I talk about several things and then she departs. Russell is wrapping up his business for the night. Sage calms the crowd down to make an announcement.

"I want to give tremendous praise to my friend Russell Davenport. I wish you great success and I look forward to more things to come from you. I know firsthand that our hometown of Linden, New Jersey is proud of you. Also, I know I can speak for all of Howard University's alumni when I say that we're proud of you. Russell, we bid you well," Sage narrates to the crowd.

Russell grabs the mic as he shakes Sage's hand and announces, "Sage, thank you. It means a lot. To all of my people from Linden, D.C., and Columbia, South Carolina, thanks a lot and just know that I'm grinding for you. I can't display through words how much it means to me. Thanks for coming out. Good night and I hope to see you all soon."

Russell and I gather our belongings and say good night to Sage and Sheena. They're a delightful couple. They get along fantastically and have two of the cutest little boys. Sage always jokes with us that things weren't always so great between he and Sheena. Sage claims that their journey to happiness is worthy of a novel or a movie. I don't know their history, but they always seem happy together.

We finally make it to the car and are on our way to the hotel. Since we hosted the book event at In the Mix, Sage was kind enough to get us the Presidential Suite at the Empire Hotel in Dupont Circle. Russell is driving and I'm feeling freaky, so I unbutton and zip down his slacks. I pull his dick out of his boxers and beat it on my lips. It starts to get hard, so I put it in my mouth. I love when his cock gets fully hard in my mouth! I spit on his dick, then I slurp on it while I suck it. Russell grabs the back of my head and presses it down. My mouth is as far down on his dick as it can possibly go and I begin to gag on it. Russell moans as my tongue and hot mouth pleasure his dick. Russell looks down at me with a look of amazement as I fondle his balls and lick the shaft of his cock. I wish I could sit on his dick right now, but I can't. I'll take care of that when we get to the hotel. Russell is so mesmerized by the head that he runs a stop sign and almost hits a car. I immediately stop sucking his dick.

"You'll just have to wait for what I have in store for you until we get stationary," I suggest.

"Girl, you know you are freaky as hell and I love it! I'm gonna tear that ass up when we get to the hotel. I hope you're ready for a marathon," Gem voices.

"I'm always ready and always will be. You just make sure your dick is ready for an all-nighter," I say confidently.

"Shit, I'm good over here. Stamina ain't never in question for me," Gem assures arrogantly.

We make it to the hotel and head inside. Gem is horny as ever after the tease I gave him on the way here. He's grabbing my luscious booty and kissing all over me as we ride the elevator to the top floor. I'm ultra horny and I feel my pussy flowing like a fire hydrant that's been busted open on a hot summer day in the hood. Gem is in for a real treat tonight. This is going to be a great way to cap off his birthday celebration. I feel Gem's dick bulging through his pants and I can't wait to put it back in my mouth. We make it to our floor and the elevator door opens, but we don't exit. We're so engulfed in our make-out session that we can't take our hands off one another. Finally, I push away from Gem, so we can really get this party started. Gem chases me into the room and can't believe his eyes.

"This is some fancy shit right here! The elevator door opens directly into our room. Sage is always hooking some extravagant shit up. That's my boy for a reason. He's always been a real classy dude. I'm gonna have to thank him again," Gem offers.

"Yass, I agree. This is a room that's fit for a king and queen. I guess that's why we're in it. In my opinion, we're on king and queen status," I reply.

"I see the champagne is on ice and it's not even melted. This is fresh ice! The hotel staff had our arrival timed just right! I love when customer service is at a premium. It's at least four separate rooms off of the main room. I don't impress easily, but I must admit, I'm beyond impressed," Gem voices enthusiastically.

"The room is beyond beautiful. As far as the champagne, I had it arranged for it to be chilled long before we arrived. Babe, you know I'm on it!" I word.

"Yes, you are on it and I have something else that you can get on! Bring your delicious self over here, so we can resume what you started in the car. Your mouth was splendid, but I want to feel your kitty purring all over my dick," Gem comments.

I zoom away from Gem and beeline to the bathroom. He knows that I have to freshen up before we get it on and popping. He follows me to the bathroom as I start stripping for my shower. To my delight, he pops me on my ass.

"Boy, don't start nothing you can't finish," I say as I turn on the faucet for the shower.

"Well, I can finish it and that's why I started. I'm gonna check out the rest of the room while you shower," Gem tells.

"Wait!" I yell out.

"What am I waiting for?" he inquires.

"I'm slightly offended. I'm ass naked in the shower and you're telling me that you'd rather go look at the hotel room. I guess I must not be that attractive if I can't compete with a room. Also, I need you to wash my back for me," I say.

"Kim, I know you better than that. You just want me in there with you and I don't have a problem with that," Gem says.

"Well, if you know so much, why do you still have your damn clothes on?" I ask.

Gem doesn't respond orally, but be does react physically. Gem takes off all of his clothes in seemingly one swoop and is in the shower with me. He gets behind me and starts washing my back, but all I feel is his dick poking me. Gem doesn't stop at washing my back. He gives me a full body cleansing. He finishes washing me and then I return the favor. We exit the shower dripping wet with towels in our hands.

I tell Gem to sit on the couch, so I can dry him off. Next, I turn on some music and pour us some champagne. The music is playing in the background and the mood is just right for a late night of passion and seduction. I guzzle my glass of wine and then I kneel down in front of him. I take the towel and start drying Gem's legs while he relaxes and sips his drink. I suck his dick as I blot the water beads off of his beautiful body. Gem grabs me by my chin as I pleasure him.

He grunts in pleasure and throws the towel away. I know he's ready to fuck me and I'm ready for him to fuck me too. His dick is standing at attention. Since his dick is standing, I sit my pussy on it. Gem wants to see my ass jiggle, so I mount him with my back to him. I place my hands on his knees to brace myself and begin gyrating on his meat. I start off fast, but Gem slows me down. I slowly pop my pussy up and down on his dick allowing him to feel all of my juices and every inch of me. Gem places one hand at the base of my back and guides my movements.

"You like that daddy?" I ask as I look back over my shoulder.

"Baby, yes! It's so wet and tight. Nice and slow just like that," Gem responds.

I continue riding him slowly as he desires.

Moments later, Gem grabs my waist firmly with both hands and demands that I go faster. I follow his orders and begin bouncing speedily up and down off of his thick brown pole. The room is filled with sounds of my ass clapping and wet pussy. The ass clapping sounds have overtaken the music we have playing.

I feel my body heating up and it begins to tingle. My nipples and clit are hardened, so I know it won't be long before I erupt. I'm almost ready to explode all over Gem's dick. I fondle my clit as Gem methodically slaps my booty. Gem orders me to sit straight up and he clutches me with both hands under my titties and begins to stroke his dick in my pussy quickly and thunderously. His strokes rub my G-spot and make my body tingle even more.

"Oh my…ooh, I'm bout cum! Right there…don't fuckin stop!" I scream out as my body tenses up.

I begin tremoring violently as I start to orgasm. I run my fingers through my hair. I rub my clit even faster than I was in a fit of extreme pleasure. All the pressure and energy I had is flushed in a blink of an eye. My body goes limp and I fall off of Gem's dick.

"I wanna taste my juices on you," I say to Gem.

Of course, Gem acquiesces because he absolutely adores my dick sucking skills and it drives him crazy when I suck him off directly after he pulls out of me. Gem loves when I turn on my freaky side. I return to my former position on my knees, so I can start sucking Gem off again. I reach down and open a pack of Halls that I stashed under the couch just for this moment. I put a Halls in my mouth and go back to work on his meat wagon.

After a few slurps on his cock, Gem feels the cooling sensation of the Halls on the head of his dick. He looks down at me with a look of stupefaction. The cooling sensation prolongs his nut, but allows him to enjoy the euphoric feeling for a longer time period. I stop sucking his dick and grab it at its base. I tickle the head of his dick with my tongue. Gem squirms because he's overridden by pleasure. I follow his every move and continue tickling and his dick's head. He demands that I start sucking it again, so I do.

However, this time it's different. Gem is in control of how I suck his dick. He tells me to sit on the couch and open wide. I promptly do as he requests and sit in position as he climbs on the couch in front of me. My lips are right by his balls, so I begin sucking them while he stands over me. Gem is stroking his dick while I give his balls lip service. A few seconds later, Gem stops me from sucking his balls and puts his dick in my mouth. My back is against the couch and Gem grips the back of my head. He pumps my mouth in long steady strokes as he grunts. Each grunt and stroke he makes, turns me on and I feel a gush of juices flow through my pussy. I grab Gem's ass and pull him vigorously. The force makes him fuck my face swiftly and I gag on his meat. Gem's ball sack is banging my chin rapidly. I drop one hand from gripping Gem's ass to play with my kitty. Gem hears the sounds of my pussy overflowing with moisture.

"It sounds like she's ready for me to put him back in her," Gem observes.

He stops stroking my mouth and jumps off the couch. I can tell that Gem's ready to get his now. I suggest that we go to the bedroom of the suite, so we can really stretch out and have a real fuck session. Gem is all for the bedroom and picks me up and carries me to it. He kisses me passionately as we stride to the room. Gem looks at me and kisses me as if I'm the only person in the world.

He gently places me on the edge of the bed. He kneels down on the floor and sensually begins licking my pussy. I close my eyes and roll my body to the direction of his tongue. Gem is a kitty licking connoisseur and is equally skilled in serving the dick. Gem stops eating me.

"How do you want it?" he asks.

I reply, "I want to try something different tonight for your birthday. Just lie down on your back and I'll take care of the rest."

"First you surprised me with the Halls. Now, you have another trick. I need to have birthdays more often," Gem speaks jokingly.

"Oh, is that right?" I ask.

Gem shoots back, "Damn right, if you're going to keep creating new stunts for us to try. You know I like to up the ante."

"Boy, you know you're a damn mess. Lie down and stop talking," I utter.

Gem lies down on his back. He's stretched across the bed stark naked. His chest is chiseled and his six pack is impeccable. His dick is pointing straight up like the antenna at the top of the Empire State Building. I want to jump on his dick and pounce on it right now, but I have to stick to the plan. I get the rope that's stashed under the bed and begin tying Gem's hands and legs to the bed posts. Next, I grab the chocolate syrup out of the frig.

Gem states, "Oh, I guess we're getting real freaky tonight…ropes and chocolate syrup! I know the head job you're going to give me is about to be mind-blowing!"

"Yes, honey. I'm going to blow your mind. That's the plan! You deserve it. You're so good to me," I say.

I tell Gem to close his eyes and wait to be pleased at the ultimate level. He does as ordered and closes his eyes. I suck his dick and he's going wild from the pleasure of it. His dick is throbbing and has so many veins in it that it looks like a road mad. I pour some of the chocolate syrup on his chest and stomach. I lick it off of him while I kiss and grope his body sensually. I climb up to Gem's face and I blanket his mouth with my pussy. I lean forward and begin sucking his dick while he eats me out in the 69 position. I fondle his balls and lick up and down his shaft. I beat his swollen dick on my face and he loves it.

I hear him moaning as his tongue invades my pussy. I sit upright on Gem's face again. His tongue is in my pussy teasing my G-Spot. I twirl in a circular motion as he tongue fucks me. While I'm riding his face, I decide that it's time for another surprise. I clap my hands three times to begin the next round of gratification. The lights go dim at my claps.

Seconds later, Gem starts going wild again as he feels glossed up succulent lips kissing along his shaft and balls. This time it's different again because they're not my lips on his dick. I'm still riding his face. I climb off of Gem's face because I know he's confused. He immediately looks down to see who's joined us tonight. When his eyes focus on who's giving him head, he realizes that it's the woman who runs *Black People Magazine*, Cassie Monroe.

"Gem, this is your last surprise of the night. I hope you aren't upset," I say.

"Umm, I'm not upset, but you didn't have to do this. I would've been perfectly fine with what we do...what we've always done," Gem replies.

"I know, but I wanted it to be extra special for you. It's your birthday and we're celebrating another book being released. Besides, you always said it was one of your fantasies, so I decided to make it happen for you," I explain sincerely.

"Wow, all of this for little ole me! I'm impressed. If you want to proceed, we can. Honey, it's totally your decision," Gem expresses.

I take a shot of tequila and so does Cassie. I sit on Gem's face after I down the shot and he continues eating me out. Cassie pours more tequila on Gem's stomach and dick then vacillates between licking it off his chest and sucking it off his dick. I never imagined that I'd be this turned on by this, but I am. This is awesome! I'm so aroused. I don't know if it's because of the masterful job Gem is doing while eating me out or if it's from watching Cassie taste Gem.

Either way, I'm soaking wet right now and I'm all smiles. I'm gyrating on Gem's face and Cassie quits giving him head. She decides it's time that she goes for a ride. She stands up on the bed and then lowers herself onto Gem's dick. She has her feet planted in the mattress as she plunges down on Gem's dick repeatedly. She's taking every inch of his dick forcefully to her pussy. I know Gem's enjoying it because he's eating my pussy more feverishly. There is a splash of pussy juices each time Cassie gets to the base of his dick. All I hear is splat, splat, splat.

Cassie shifts her position, so we hold hands to give her balance. She really goes wild once she's sure not to fall. Gem starts pumping his waist to maximize his penetration into Cassie's pussy and it's working. Her grip on my hands gets stronger every time Gem thrusts into her. She's screaming loudly in pleasure while Gem grunts and moans.

"It's so deep! So fuckin deep!" Cassie screams as she grabs her stomach. "This is some good black dick!"

"I know... That's why I can't get enough of it!" I reply.

"Girl, I know that's right!" Cassie remarks.

Cassie becomes winded or just can't take the deep penetration that Gem provides and takes her feet from under her. She continues riding Gem, but is now slowly taking the dick. She's running her hands through her hair as she gracefully gallops on his raging bull. Gem is still licking my pussy. Cassie and I are facing each other as she rides his dick and I ride his face. I reach forward and caress her supple titties. She responds with a smirk of enjoyment and licks her lips.

She leans forward and so do I. I nuzzle her boobs then stick my tongue out and begin licking her nipples. Cassie squeezes her tits as I lick them. We begin kissing as Gem is serving Cassie his slong and serving me his tongue. Cassie starts kissing me harder and locks her hands on both of my shoulders and starts pumping Gem's dick fast again. Cassie lets out a high-pitched moan of excitement and goes into violent convulsions as she releases her juices on Gem.

She laughs in incredibility of how hard Gem

made her cum. I climb down off of Gem's face. He expresses that he wants to be in control since we jumped him. We untie Gem and become his willing subjects. Gem tells me to lie on my back and spread my legs, so I get in position. He orders Cassie to bend over and start tasting me. Her lips feel softer on my pussy than they did on my face. It feels like my clit is a treasure chest and her lips are the keys to unlock all of my inhibitions. While Cassie is bent over, Gem starts fucking her from the back. He has the bottle of tequila in his hand and sips it while he slowly strokes her.

I see Gem is enjoying himself. Gem normally becomes a real animal sexually when he sips tequila. I hope tonight is no different. Cassie is handling Gem's strokes like a champ as she swirls her tongue around my clit and subtly kisses my pussy lips. She's also fingering me while she tastes me which adds another level of delight. Gem plants his feet firmly and begins pounding Cassie's kitty from the back. Cassie is getting manhandled and screams.

"Fuck this pussy then, dammit! Fuck me!" Cassie yells out.

Cassie pulls me closer to her and buries her face in my pussy. She concentrates her tongue efforts on my clit while she caresses my G-spot with her finger. It feels so good that I try to run from it, but I can't because she has me locked down. Since I can't run, I grab her head and enjoy her eating skills. She's making her tongue roll in waves and the sensation on my clit is driving me wild. I've never felt anything like this before. I arch my back while she's eating me as I feel myself about to orgasm. My heart is beating fast and I feel a huge gush shoot out of my body. I squirt a white milky substance all over Cassie's face. Simultaneously, Gem starts to pull out of Cassie's pussy and shoots a heavy load of cum all over her ass.

I want to taste Gem's nut, so I jump up and grab his dick. I put it in my mouth, so I can taste his nut mixed with Cassie's juices. Cassie is a freak like me. She kisses me and sucks my tongue to taste herself and Gem cum. Gem moans loudly and squirms from the overwhelmingly pleasurable feeling.

CHAPTER 4

It's been a very busy month since Gem's birthday and book release celebration. We've been in different cities doing book promotions seemingly every night. However, I'm not surprised that it's going this way because we always get extremely busy when Gem releases a new book. Living in hotels for extended periods of time is for the birds. I just want to curl up in my bed and throw my own covers over my head. I swear I could fall asleep for twenty-four hours straight.

I'm living the life of a best-selling author's wife. I guess I have to take the good with the bad. Honestly, the good far outweighs the bad. We just arrived at our hotel in Columbia, South Carolina. We're here to attend a book festival that they have every year at a local convention center. Gem was a vendor at this same event a few years back and was shown a tremendous amount of support from the city while here. We come back to their book fair every year to show our appreciation for the love we were previously shown, but we weren't planning to attend this year and then things changed. This year is different than years past because Gem is a featured author and will be speaking on a panel at the book fair. Also, he's going to Irmo High School to be a judge of their annual Poetry Slam Competition. Additionally, he'll be guest hosting a radio show on the local radio station. Our schedule will really be jammed packed while we're here. I'm not complaining because if we're staying busy, it means we're trending.

Gem lets me out of the car directly in front of the hotel. I get out of the car and walk inside to get us checked into the room. Gem stays with the car to take care of the unloading and parking of the vehicle. As soon as I get to the counter to check-in, my phone begins to ring. I pull the phone out of my pocket to investigate who's calling me. It's Cassie Monroe calling. She's been calling frequently ever since our encounter a month ago. I have to get checked in, so I don't answer the call. I'll call her back later when time permits.

The service at the hotel is stellar and we're immediately checked in. Simultaneously, Gem is walking through the hotel lobby doors with the bellhops. They follow us up to our room and drop our luggage. The room is nice, but not nearly as nice as the room at the Empire Suites that Sage booked for us. It'll get the job done for the short time we're here. Gem tips the bellhops and they depart. We unpack some of our clothes and then head down to the bar in the hotel. We'll have some cocktails while we devise a plan for all we have to do in Columbia. Gem and I make it to the bar and notice that the bar also sells food, so we decide to eat here too. There's no need to travel somewhere else to eat. Gem's phone chimes alerting him to a text message. He reads the message.

"Damn, it's Cassie Monroe again. She called me when we first got to the hotel, but I was busy with the bellhop, so I didn't answer," Gem states.

"Yeah, she obviously called us at pretty much the same time because she called me while I was checking in. I was unable to answer as well. I'll hit her back soon," I speak.

"Gotcha I did send her a text back though. I let her know that I was busy and would reach out to her at my earliest convenience," Gem words.

"Oh, okay. Well, why the hell is she still texting you? What does the new message say?" I inquire.

"Nothing of any substance," Gem answers.

He slides his phone over to me, so I can read it for myself. The message just asks him to get in touch with her as soon as possible and she looks forward to hearing from him soon. I don't know if I should be offended by Cassie's message or not. I don't know if her message is loaded or truly innocent. There's no telling these days. I know we had a fun night, but I hope she isn't going overboard. Maybe I'm tripping because she did call both of us.

"Gem, do me a favor," I say.

Gem voices, "Anything you want is alright with me. You know that. Just tell me what the favor is and it's done."

"Thank you Honey. Listen, if Cassie reaches out to you again, do one of two things for me. Either don't respond at all or let her know to contact me directly. I think it'll be better to handle it this way going forward," I articulate.

"Say no more. Your wish is my command. Enough of Cassie though. I'm ready to eat. We have to order something now," Gem utters while rubbing his stomach. "A brother is hungry!"

The bartender brings us our drinks and we order some food. Gem guzzles his first drink and quickly orders another one. About twenty minutes later, our food comes out and is piping hot just the way Gem likes it. He attacks the food before the bartender even has a chance to fully sit the plate down. Halfway through the meal, Gem orders another drink and so do I. While we're eating, we hear a familiar female's voice from afar.

She says, "Well, if it isn't my favorite couple!"

Gem and I are both overtaken by a range of emotions. We both recognize the voice as being

Cassie Monroe's, but we are both shocked and puzzled. We can't imagine why she'd be in our hotel hundreds of miles from D.C. We don't know if we should be scared or not. All we know is that this is stalker-like to us. Maybe we should just get up from the bar and run. Gem plays it cool even though his eyes are telling me how he truly feels. He fixes his facial expression to one of delight and turns in the direction of Cassie to greet her.

"Cassie, hello. What's up? How are you?" Gem asks.

"I'm fine. How are you two doing?" Cassie inquires.

I answer, "We're fine. I can speak for my husband and me when I say that you're the last person we expected to see here!"

"Seriously, I couldn't believe my ears when I heard your voice," Gem offers.

Cassie replies, "I totally understand because when I saw you two I couldn't believe my eyes. I thought that my eyes had to be playing tricks on me."

"Your eyes didn't deceive you and our ears didn't deceive us," Gems says.

"Well, we all know that we're here, but the real question is for you Cassie. What are you doing here?" I inquire emphatically.

"I'm here for the book festival this weekend. I come or one of my representatives comes every year. A lot of women of color frequent the event, so it's perfect for my magazine. I always make plenty of solid connections while at this event while also affording my magazine plenty of exposure," Cassie explains.

"Oh, well that explains it. When we heard you call out, we were stunned for a moment. We didn't know why you'd be here at the same hotel as us. Well, as you probably surmised, we're here for the book festival as well. Gem is a featured author this year and will be presenting on how to build suspense in writing," I orate.

"Yeah, I figured as much when I saw you. It's one hell of a coincidence! That's great Gem! I see you're just great at everything you do," Cassie remarks as she winks at Gem.

"Yes, he is," I comment.

"Don't I know it. Well, I just came to say hello when I saw you guys. I won't interrupt your evening any further. Enjoy your night and maybe I'll see you two at the convention center tomorrow," Cassie responds. "I hope to hear you speak tomorrow!"

Gem says, "Alright... Good seeing you too! I'll be presenting tomorrow at noon in ballroom A."

"Good night Cassie. Oh wait, before you go... I missed a call from you," I voice.

"Yes, I can't believe I almost forgot. I have great news for you!" Cassie words in an exuberant tone.

I tell Cassie to have a seat to tell us all about

this good news that she's clearly very excited about. I figure that with how crazy things have been lately, that we better speak now while we have some time. Cassie informs us that she spoke to one of her friends in the movie industry. She claims that she told him about Gem's series and he's intrigued about turning the book series into a television series. Of course, Gem and I are all ears. We order more drinks while Cassie fills us in on all of the details.

"Now, nothing is written in stone, but I think this is a step in the right direction for you guys," Cassie comments.

We finish dinner, drinks, and conversing about the interview, magazine cover, and a myriad of other things. It's time to shut it down. We all need our rest for tomorrow. Gem pays the tab and we head to the elevator to get to our room. We are staying on a higher floor than Cassie, so we reach her floor first. We've all had a good bit to drink, so Gem suggests that we walk Cassie to her room door to ensure she makes it safely. I don't have a problem with it, so we make our way to her room.

"Service with a smile," Gem says as we stand in front of her door.

"Well, I thank you for walking me to my door, but I was hoping for the full-service treatment tonight," Cassie says as she caresses her boobs.

"Is that right, Cassie? What do you think Gem?" I ask.

"Well, we are all here. It seems like an act of fate brought us together again tonight," he answers. "Kim, ultimately, if you like it, I love it!"

I don't respond to Gem. Actions speak louder than words, so I grab Cassie by her ass cheeks and we go into her room. Cassie goes to freshen up as soon as we enter her room. I fix Gem and myself drinks while we wait. I suck his dick as he sits in the office chair. Moments later, while I'm still sucking Gem's dick, I notice it's not as hard as it was when I initially started sucking him off. I look up at Gem and his eyes are closed and he's knocked out in a drunken stupor. I know I shouldn't have let him drink so much tonight.

Cassie comes out of the bathroom and sees Gem is unconscious. She's at a loss for words. She didn't expect to see Gem this way. I didn't either. I tell her that Gem and I can just leave since tonight isn't a good time.

"I was really in the mood tonight for some action, but I understand if you have to leave," Cassie says.

"Girl, yasss! I know what you mean. I'm in the mood for some action too. Hell, our night doesn't have to end because Gem can't participate. We can have a very satisfying night with just you and me," I suggest.

Cassie voices, "Oh, I don't know about that. Gem would probably be upset if he found out about us doing this without him. I don't want to jeopardize our future business deals."

"Girl bye! You can miss me with all of that Gem talk. He's my husband and I know him better than anyone. He's not the insecure type. He's firm in his position and won't feel slighted if we proceed without him. It's not our fault that he went to sleep. Besides, he was fully onboard with what was going to happen before he passed out. Hell, he basically left us hanging. If anyone should be mad, it should be us," I explain. "All this liquor that's in me has me hot and bothered. Hell, I ned to release now!"

"Well, I can't argue that. He's your man and he did leave us hanging. This liquor is talking to me too, so if you think it's okay, I'm ready to get it on," Cassie utters as her slightly damp body glistens.

I yank Cassie's towel off of her and expose her naked and slightly moist body. Her brown nipples are erect and her kitty is shaved bald. I caress her naked body as she caresses mine. We kiss each other passionately as we dance to the music. Her body smells like cinnamon and tastes like vanilla. We dance over to the bar to have another drink. Cassie and I sit down on the barstools and take shots of tequila. I kneel down if front of Cassie's barstool and part her legs. Her pussy is an unblemished canvas. Her lips are juicy and alluring, so I lick them. I spread her lips apart and behold her pristine pink pussy. Her kitty is pink like freshly made cotton candy. I lick her in and around her pussy and she tastes even sweeter than cotton candy.

"Yasss, Kim! I like that! You know what mommy likes. Ooh, don't stop," Cassie voices seductively as she fondles her clit and runs her fingers through my hair.

Cassie cums in my mouth as her body goes into convulsions. She has her legs locked around my head as she releases. Cassie laughs from the extreme jubilation I've given her. We change positions. I'm on the barstool and Cassie's on the floor. Now it's my turn to let off some steam. Cassie wants to taste me from the back, so she orders me to bend over and brace myself on the barstool. I happily oblige. Cassie licks and sucks my pussy from the back. I push my booty back on her face as she pleases me. As she eats my pussy, she tickles my asshole with her finger and the unexpected sensation is delightful. I'm feeling euphoria that I never experienced before. I grab the barstool chair tightly as I tremor violently while I cum. In my weakened state, I gently crumble to the floor and can't move.

Eventually, I rise from the floor and go clean myself up. When I exit the bathroom, Cassie is resting in the bed in a black lingerie set. Gem's still asleep and I'm ill prepared to carry him upstairs to our suite, so we'll be sleeping here tonight. I crawl into bed with Cassie. We converse for a while and eventually fall asleep.

"Kim! Kim, wake up!" Gem yells as I wake up

groggily. "Kim, it's time to get upstairs, so we can get ready for the book festival!"

"What time is it? I didn't oversleep, did I?" I ask wildly as I get up in a panic.

"It's seven-thirty. No, you didn't oversleep, but we need to get going if we're going to be on time," Gem states.

Gem pulls the cover back and sees Cassie under the covers in her lingerie set. He looks at me with a devilish grin after he sees her. Cassie wakes up as I put my clothes on and gather my things.

"Good morning, Russell. I'm sorry I missed out on feeling you inside of me last night," Cassie states.

Russell replies, "I'm sorry too. That liquor whooped my ass last night. It looks like I missed out on another epic night. There's always next time."

"Well, I'll be looking forward to it," Cassie comments.

I remark, "Sounds like a plan!"

Russell speaks, "Okay, well we have to get a move on. Let's go Kim."

We tell her that we'll see her later and we depart.

CHAPTER 5

The book festival in Columbia, SC was a huge success. Gem was dazzling during his speaking engagement and really had the crowd and interviewers eating out of the palm of his hand. All of his obligations that weekend were executed as planned. He really flourished during the radio interview. He was so captivating that people were literally coming up to the radio station to meet him and buy copies of his novels. Needless to say, we sold every copy of the novels we brought to Columbia. We'll definitely be in Columbia for business again in the future. Honestly, it was great being able to mix business with pleasure while there.

I figured that we'd have an extremely busy time in Columbia and would be tired upon our return, so I didn't schedule anything for Gem and I to do this week. Gem is planning to start his next novel this week and I'll make a few calls to set some things up down the road, but we're not doing anything too strenuous. One thing that I am doing is going to the nail salon and spa today. I messed up two of my nails while in Columbia over the weekend and it was all Gem's fault. He's treating me to the spa for a full body massage as well as a manicure and pedicure.

I yell to Gem, "Let's go baby! My appointment is at three and it's already two thirty! You know I'm not trying to be late."

"Kim, relax. It only takes ten minutes to get there, so you'll be there early. I really don't see why I'm going with you anyway. You can drive yourself," Gem voices.

I respond, "Umm, you're driving me because you're treating me today. Remember you said today is all about me, so stop. Also, don't forget you're the reason why my nails need to be redone to begin with. Besides that, you know you love me to pieces and want nothing more than to spend the day pampering me."

"I'll take the blame for your nails to some degree, but don't fill yourself up with this narrative that I want to be around you all day," Gem replies jokingly. "I really don't like your ass like that anyway."

Gem has jokes, I see. I grab a pillow off of the couch and throw it at him. He ducks out of the way of the pillow and laughs. I chase him around the couch and through the living room, but I can't catch him. He's way faster than me, but I'll get him back later for his joke. Surely, he'll let his guard down and it'll be on like popcorn.

"For someone who doesn't like my ass, you surely were all up in it last night!" I shoot back while rolling my neck.

"Damn, right I was and I'm gonna get back in it tonight after we finish running around. Last night won't compare to tonight," Gem remarks.

I can't wait for tonight because I know Gem will deliver on his promise. Each time we make love is better than the time before it. I used to hear all the time how couples reach their sexual peak and used to think Gem and I would fall victim to the same curse, but that's not our reality. Gem won't allow things to get stale and amazes me every time we do the damn thang!

"Well, you know I'll be waiting for you to show me what you're ranting about!" I say.

Gem and I leave to go to the nail salon. To my delight, we're in and out of there in no time. After the fact, I'm glad Gem was complicit in breaking my nails because these new nails are much better than the last. I hope my spa treatment affords me the same level of satisfaction as these nails are giving me. I don't play... I slay!!! We arrive at the spa facility and I get checked in. I go in the back to get undressed while Gem chills in the lobby. Ninety minutes later, I emerge from the spa treatment area.

"How was it? Do you feel relaxed?" Gem

asks.

"Yes, honey! Oh, my goodness! I had to have fallen asleep like three times! That was heaven! Baby, thank you so much," I speak happily as I give Gem a kiss.

"You're welcome. I'm glad you enjoyed it! You deserve it!" Gem comments.

"I needed it too. As good as you make love to me, I would never imagine that I'd still be so tense, but a full body massage is different from an all-out sex session," I verbalize.

"You're right about that! Check this out. You'll never guess who's here right now," Gem states.

"Morris Chestnut? No wait…Boris Kodjoe? Who?" I ask frantically.

"No, if they were here, I wouldn't be telling your ass. You are so damn crazy!" Gem replies while laughing. "Your girl is here!"

"My girl? Who the hell is my girl?" I inquire.

"Cassie Monroe!" Gem answers.

"Gem, please tell me your ass is playing! Ain't no damn way!" I word in a shocked tone.

"Kim, I'm dead ass serious! As soon as you were called back, I went outside to make a few calls and she was walking in as I was walking out. She's back there now. I'm surprised you didn't see her," Gem offers.

I utter, "Wow! All I can say is wow! Baby, this can't just be another coincidence. It's too much. I mean this is way too much!"

"Now, you know that I'm not one for conspiracy theories, but when I saw her walking in, I said to myself that this is weird. Coincidences don't just happen like this with the same person. Hell no!" Gem articulates.

"I know you aren't a conspiracy theorist, but I agree, this is a bit much. Think about it like this… We'd never seen her before your birthday/book release party and now, all of a sudden, she's everywhere we go," I narrate.

"Right! Right! We might have a stalker on our hands. Hindsight is twenty-twenty and now I'm thinking about how she even got into In the Mix that night. She may have sought us out even before that night," Gem communicates.

"Oh my goodness! This is unbelievable! At a bare minimum, we turned her out that night we had the tryst with her. She popped up at In the Mix, the hotel out of state, and now she's here at the spa. Babe, this is some shit for one of your books," I orate.

"Hell yeah, this is novel worthy," Gem says.

"What do you want to do about it? Do you think we need to call the authorities?" I ask.

"Hmm. I don't think it's like that just yet. She's only popped up on us a few times, but she's not harassing us or anything like that, so we really would have no basis for calling the cops. If we're wrong, we could tarnish her reputation and I don't want to do that to her," Gem explains.

"You're right… She's only been friendly and

helpful, so I'll follow your lead on this. However, if she begins calling profusely or if I feel an air of violence, I'm calling the police," I tell Gem sternly.

"Trust me, if it gets slightly out of hand, I'll call the cops myself. You won't have to. We're not having any fatal attraction bullshit going on," Gem assures.

"Okay, as long as we are on the same page. I sure hope that threesome wasn't a bad idea," I state.

"Honey, we're always on the same page. You know how we do. I'm sure the threesome will blow over and continue to be a great memory we have together," Gem replies.

Gem and I are at the counter waiting to pay when Cassie comes from the spa treatment area. She greets me with a hug and we discuss how we keep running into each other. The conversation is very light-hearted and jovial. Cassie is like her normal self. We don't let on that something is unusual to us about the way we keep meeting up. Gem pays the bill and we leave. As we're pulling out of the parking lot, Cassie is exiting the spa and is waving goodbye to us. We wave back and turn onto the street.

Gem doesn't give anymore conversation to Cassie and her stalker-like ways. Instead, he bounces some ideas for his new book off of me. We drive to the outlets for some retail therapy. I've been eyeing a new handbag and I'm finally going to get it! After we shop, we drive to In the Mix for some cocktails and dinner. As we go inside, we see Sage is here as usual and greets us warmly. We're beginning to think he never leaves this place. We joke back and forth about it and come to the conclusion that we've never been here and not seen Sage.

Our dinner and cocktails come to an end, so we go home. I'm very excited to get home to see what Gem has in store for me sexually. He claimed earlier that he's going to put it down and I plan to hold him to his promise. We make it home and I beeline to the shower. When I exit the shower, Gem has candles burning and soft music playing. To my surprise, Gem has already showered in the other bathroom and is butt naked. He has a doughnut draped around his dick with caramel drizzled all over him. I laugh to myself because his dick is too thick for the doughnut hole and is ripped. I know that I'm in for an interesting night.

CHAPTER 6

Gem and I are going for a morning run. Unfortunately, we're normally busy throughout the week and don't get to take early morning runs. With such a light schedule this week, it only makes sense that we take advantage of the situation. Most of the time, we have to settle for running on the treadmill in our workout room because it's convenient and time is not normally abundant. It's not that running on the treadmill doesn't get the job done because it does, but in our opinions, running on the treadmill pales in comparison to jogging through the park. It's something about being outside and being one with nature that feels better than running indoors. I think I even breathe better while running outside.

"Gem! Gem!" I yell upstairs.

"Why are you calling my name like

something's going on?" Gem inquires sternly.

"I'm ready to go and I just didn't want you to be waiting for me," I answer.

"Oh, okay. I'll be ready in a few minutes. Just need to brush my teeth," Gem speaks.

The truth is that I really was rushing Gem. I'm trying to get to Rock Creek Park to run as soon as possible. Traffic is hell in D.C. Leaving the house even five minutes later can change the traffic tremendously. What is a quick drive with no traffic can quickly become time consuming. I'm not trying to do all that. Also, the running trail tends to get extremely crowded as it gets later in the day. I like jogging with space because I abhor having to dodge person after person while we jog.

Gem comes down stairs in a timely fashion as he said he would. We drive over to Rock Creek Park. To my delight, traffic wasn't heavy, so we arrived relatively quickly. We park the car and head over to the running trail. Gem and I stretch and complete some warmup exercises. We get our playlists set and begin running. Not many people are out here, so we run freely. Gem and I even sprint for a half mile without interruption.

Forty-five minutes later, we stop to catch our breath. After a few minutes, Gem walks off the path to the exercise apparatuses they have stationed around the path. I'm not doing any extra exercises, so I stay seated on the bench and watch Gem workout. He's working out on the pull-up bar and I'm enjoying every second of it. He has his shirt off and is sweating heavily. His slightly muscular body is glistening from the sunlight reflecting on his beads of sweat. His abs are tight and he's grunting with every pull-up he does. It kind of reminds me of when he lifts me in the air when he fucks me. I need to stop thinking about him sexually before my kitty gets moist.

I look away from Gem because I hear some joggers heading towards me. Here comes the morning rush. I'm glad we beat them here because I would be highly upset having to brush shoulders with all of those people. As the group of people gets closer, I have to do a double take because I know I don't see what I think I see. Hell, I know my eyes aren't playing tricks on me. What the hell is going on here? I jump up from the bench and zoom over to Gem.

I command, "Gem, get down! I need you to see something now!"

"See what?" Gem asks.

"Look at the people running and tell me that I'm not losing my mind. Please tell me that I'm not tripping," I voice.

Gem jumps down from the pull-up bar and starts walking over to the track to see what I'm making a fuss over. I stop him immediately and tell him to just watch from where we are. Gem observes the crowd of runners and walkers coming in our direction. He finally sees what I see.

"Oh, hell no! You got to be fucking kidding me!" Gem states in amazement.

I verbalize angrily, "Right! Fucking Cassie again! Gem, that bitch is stalking us! I know I'm not crazy."

"She's definitely stalking us! It ain't that much damn coincidence in the world. She's everywhere we are. I'm not letting this one slide. I'm going to say something to her. Fuck that!" Gem articulates.

"Honey, wait! She's a woman and so am I. I'll handle this for us. I can't have you out here going back and forth with some female. Besides, you're a public figure and we can't take the chance of your conversation with her going viral. You know someone will definitely record the incident. We have to protect your image," I narrate.

"Damn, I didn't even consider all of that. You're definitely right. I'd lose my entire female fan base if they saw me arguing with a woman. I'd never sell another book to a woman again. We'd be finished. That's why you're in charge of all of the media and public relations stuff," Gem responds.

"That's right, so I'll go talk to her and see what's going on," I say.

"Okay, just be careful. Listen, remember what you learned in that kickboxing class. Don't let her beat your ass. If it turns physical and she starts to get the best of you, I'm gonna have to defend you. Camera or no camera," Gem replies jokingly.

"Boy bye! Ain't nobody worried about her. I'll beat her little ass," I orate confidently.

I walk down to the path as I stare at Cassie. She makes eye contact with me and walks over to me. I don't want to stop her from getting her cardio in for the day, so I walk with her. I don't jump right into the problem I have with her because I don't want to be rude. I just make small talk, but the conversation is forced. Before we have a chance to talk, Cassie's phone rings.

"Kim, please excuse me. I have to take this call. I've been waiting for it for two days," Cassie states as she engages the call.

I wait for a moment, but I can tell that her conversation is going to be a while, so I just wave goodbye and walk away. I know Gem's going to be upset that I didn't get to set her straight, but I didn't see the best opportunity to have a stern conversation with her. I walk back over to Gem and I can tell from the look on his face that he's not pleased.

"What?" I ask shamefully.

"Now unless I'm tripping, there's no way you talked to her that fast. It looked like you two were best friends or some shit," Gem speaks in a frustrated tone.

I state apologetically, "I didn't get to speak to her about popping up every place we go. I tried to ease into it. I didn't want to be abrupt because people tend to shut down or become confrontational when you do that."

"I hear you, but sometimes you have to take the politically correct gloves off and get a little nasty with people. This wasn't one of those times to use your soft skills," Gem shoots back.

I hate when Gem gets at me, especially when he's right. He doesn't come for me often, but when he does, it stings. This one stings real bad. I bury my head in Gem's sweaty chest and apologize to him. He has every right to be upset with me because I told him that I'd handle it and neglected to do so. He wraps his arms around me and tells me that he's not mad, but he does emphasize the urgency of the situation. As we walk back to the car, Gem talks me to death about how crazy it is that Cassie is stalking us.

Gem voices, "To some degree, this is all my fault!"

"How do you figure that this situation is your fault, Love? You don't want to blame me for all of this bullshit?" I inquire.

"Honey, I don't blame you... I blame myself because I shouldn't have fucked her so good. I should've only given her half and we would be clear of her shenanigans," Gem tells.

I ask, "Boy, how you figure it's you she's stalking? You do know it could be me that she's interested in, right? And what the hell should you have given her half of?"

"The reason I know it's me she wants is because I gave her my entire dick. See, when a man gives a woman his whole dick while fucking, he messes her head up. I knew that before we had the threesome, but the alcohol took over," Gem explains.

I remark, "You men are full of yourselves! I bet you and the rest of the male population really think that shit is true. I can't believe you said that. I've never heard anything so outrageously ridiculous in my entire life. I can't…I can't with you."

"I'm trying to tell you it's true," Gem replies. "My dick is too damn good!"

Gem's phone rings and halts our conversation. I'm not at all upset that our conversation is interrupted because I was done hearing about the "whole dick theory". I have much better things to do with my time than to listen to that foolishness. I'm just glad Gem isn't mad at me anymore. I don't like disappointment on my man's face. That's a no-no! Gem finishes his phone call as we're pulling up to our home.

"Baby, I'm going to call Cassie to setup a meeting. I told you I'll handle it and I will," I voice.

"That's cool. I think that's a good idea. Shit, even if you two don't meet up, you can still hash it out over the phone," Gem comments.

I call Cassie, but she doesn't answer, so I leave a message for her to call me back. She's a busy woman, but I hope she responds to my message in a timely fashion. Gem and I shower and partake in a midday quickie. After the quickie, Gem goes to his office to write for a while. He writes at some of the weirdest times of the day. He'll be relaxing one minute and the next, he'll be writing feverishly. I make a few calls for some promo events I want Gem to attend. Hours later, Gem urgently walks into the living room where I'm sitting.

"Look at this shit!" Gem orders.

He passes me his phone to inspect it. To my disliking, he has a text message from Cassie. The message states that she needs to talk to him immediately. She hasn't responded to my call, but she manages to text Gem. This is the shit that I don't like. She has no reason to text my man especially after I called her.

"She hasn't even responded to my call yet, but she's texting you! I don't like that!" I yell.

"That's what I'm saying. She actually called before she texted me, but I didn't answer because you said you wanted to handle it," Gem reports.

"Since she can call and text you, I'll just call her from your phone!" I communicate.

I decide to take the gloves off. Hell, no more soft pedaling for me. I'm going to give this thot bitch a piece of my mind right now. The nerve of her calling and texting my man, but won't respond my call. Oh, hell no! It's not going down like that at all! I dial her number back and it rings twice.

"Hello, Russell, thanks for calling me back," Cassie utters quickly as she answers the phone. "We need to talk."

I respond, "No, bitch. This is Cassie! And why..."

The line goes dead before I finish my sentence. Cassie hung up on me. She clearly doesn't want to talk to me because she knows that I now know that she's after my man. Gem is standing near me and is shocked when I inform him that Cassie hung up on me. He wants me to call her back and I comply. Not surprisingly, she doesn't answer the phone.

"Your girl is off the hook," Gem says.

"That is not my girl, so stop saying that! I don't want her calling and texting you when she won't talk to me! I'm blocking her ass from hitting your phone. If she wants to talk to anyone, it'll be to me. Fuck the bullshit!" I convey.

"Damn right! Block her ass cause I don't want her crazy ass trying to talk to me. I don't need that drama in my life. If I would've known all of this was gonna happen, I never would've consented to the threesome," Gem assures.

"I know that's right!" I reply.

Before I block her, I send her a text telling her to stop calling and texting Gem. Gem tells me that he wants to get back to his writing, so I leave him to it. I go to conduct some business on the computer and then prepare dinner for us. A while later, Gem emerges from his office and joins me in the kitchen. Dinner is ready and it's time to eat. Gem and I enjoy a stuffed chicken dinner with mashed potatoes and green beans. After dinner, we retire for the night.

Damn, what time is it? I reach over to my nightstand to grab my phone. I move my hand around in the darkness until I feel my phone. As I grab my phone, I hit the button that illuminates it and almost blind myself.

"Oh my goodness!" I yell out as I turn the phone away from my face to avoid its brightness.

I know Gem is going to wake up any second now. Any time I roll over in the bed he wakes up to check on me. If he hasn't had anything to drink, he sleeps very lightly. I wait a few seconds, but Gem doesn't make any comments or even roll over. I extend my hand to his side of the bed, but can't reach him. Obviously, he's sleeping at the edge of his side of the bed and that's why I can't reach him. Come to think of it, I don't even hear him breathing. I press the button on my phone to light it up and point it to Gem's side of the bed.

To my surprise, Gem is not in the bed. Where the hell is he? I didn't notice him getting up from bed. Either I was in a comatose-like slumber or he snuck out of bed. I immediately sit up in the bed. I don't see any light illuminating from the master bathroom, so I know he isn't in there. I'm losing my mind.

"Gem," I call out softly because I don't want to startle him.

Unfortunately, Gem doesn't answer. I shine my phone light over to his nightstand to see if his phone is sitting on it, but it's not. Now, I'm starting to get worried. I get up off the bed and go into the bathroom. It's possible Gem is using the bathroom while listening to music. He's done that a thousand times before. I call Gem's name again and get the same result as the first time. I hear a noise downstairs, so I head down. Now, why is Gem not answering me? I'm sure he heard me call his name or at least has heard me stirring about.

My hands are beginning to tremble with anger. I know Gem is downstairs laughing at me. He knows how my nerves get. I'm going to wring his neck. I make my way to the top of the staircase and look down. Shockingly, there are no lights on downstairs either. What the hell is he doing down there in the dark?

"Gem, stop playing around down there and answer me. Your ass plays way too much! You're starting to make me get angry and afraid," I speak out loudly.

Again, Gem doesn't respond at all. Now, Gem loves a good joke, but this is unlike him to carry a joke this far once he knows I'm becoming worried and perturbed. I turn on the light and look downstairs. Everything seems to be in order, so I walk downstairs. As I'm walking downstairs, I call Gem's phone. Gladly, I faintly hear his phone ringing. The ringing is coming from the direction of his office. I breathe a sigh of relief as I approach his office. Sometimes when Gem can't sleep, he'll go to his office and use the opportunity to write in his journal or to pen another book. He must really be locked into what he's working on because he isn't picking up the phone. I swear this man has tunnel vision when he gets into his work. I admire the way he focuses in on his passion.

I make it to his office and open the door. His office light is on and his phone is sitting on his desk, but he's not in here. What the fuck is going on? I storm out of the office to investigate what's going on.

"Russell! Russell! Where the hell are you?" I yell out angrily.

As I'm calling out for Russell, I hear a car starting from in front of the house. I grab my car keys and hurry to the front door and see Russell in the car. Where in the world is he going this time of night? Why did he leave his phone behind and why did he not tell me? See, this is the type of shit I don't like! All he had to do was tell me he was going somewhere. I run out the door and jump in my car to follow him.

Russell makes a left off of our block and drives straight. I hope he continues straight for a while because that will make following him easier for me. If he makes a bunch of turns, it'll be easy for him to notice me trailing him. If he stays straight, I can follow him from a distance. My mind is racing a thousand miles per second. I really can't figure out where he would be going this time of night. I want to stay optimistic about his movements, but my intuition is telling me that something underhanded is in the makes.

Russell never leaves home without his phone. There's been times when Russell left his phone home and turned around to get it. This route he's driving is unusual to me. There are no coffee shops or eateries even in this direction. Damn it! He just made a turn. I hope he doesn't make another turn off of that street. If he does, I'll lose him for sure. I should've followed him more closely. I followed too far back and now I have to speed up dramatically.

I make it to the corner he turned at, but I have no sight of his vehicle. I drive urgently, but meticulously also. I slow down at each intersection and visually inspect the streets to see if I see a car or a person moving. Angrily, I don't see any cars or anything in motion. I don't see any lights or anything. Damn it! I lost him! What the hell am I going to do now? I guess I'll go home and wait for him to get back. That's not really what I want to do, but I have no other choice. I absolutely abhor being passive and waiting for things to happen.

I know I'm going to be wide awake until he

comes home, so it doesn't even make sense to go home right now. Hell, he had to turn down one of these streets. I'll just drive down each and every one of them until I see his car. What do I have to lose? I know Gem better not come home later and tell me that he went somewhere to write another story. I'm not falling for that this time. There is absolutely nowhere for him to write in this upscale residential neighborhood. I slowly drive up and down several blocks, but I'm not having any luck.

Alright, I guess it's time to call it quits. I could be searching all night and still not find him. Besides, I'm tired as hell. The last thing I need or want is to crash into one of these parked cars. I know one thing and it's that Gem is going to have hell to pay when he gets home. I will not stand for this type of behavior. There's only one thing he could be doing at this time of night around here. I'm becoming more and more infuriated as I picture what Gem is doing.

Tears are steadily streaming down my face. Each drop burns my eyes like they're filled with molten lava. My heart is pounding out of my chest like someone's beating on a drum. As I get more and more upset, my foot presses the gas pedal harder and harder. My vision is becoming blurred from the burning sensation in my eyes. I know I need to stop, but I can't because I'm overtaken by rage. The thought of what Gem is doing right now has me unable to use my better judgment.

I'm driving so fast that I run a stop sign because I just didn't see it. I made several turns in this neighborhood to the point that I've lost my way. I'm going to have to use GPS to guide me home. As I drive erratically, I type my home address into my phone's GPS. I zoom down the street in complete oblivion. I look at the screen on my phone and notice that my GPS is indicating that I need to turn around.

I'm puzzled as to why the GPS is telling me to turn around. I reduce my speed as I look to my left and right. I realize that I'm driving the wrong direction down a one-way street. My current state of rage has me disconnection from reason. I stop my car completely and take several deep breaths. I have to gain control of my actions before I kill myself or some innocent bystander. I really just lost it. I know I'm better than this.

After several deep breaths and a moment of sitting still, I have control of myself. There are no more tears of lava burning my eyes and my breathing and thinking have returned to normal. I need to turn around and drive the proper direction down this street. I chuckle out loud as I pull into a driveway to make a K-turn. As I complete my K-turn, my headlights shine brightly on all the cars parked near me.

To my surprise, one of the cars that is illuminated is Russell's. How fortunate is this? My reckless driving and being out of control is what enabled me to find Russell's car. I should slash all of his damn tires or break his windshield. There's no way he can explain being in this neighborhood at this time of night. My thoughts are negatively impacting my emotions because my heart is starting to pound again. I can't lose control again. It's just not worth it for a dishonest man.

However, I will catch him in the act. I park my car down the street from where Russell is parked and walk back to his car. I don't have his car key with me, but I do know the code for the door keypad. I walk to the driver's side door of the car and enter the code. The door unlocks and I get in the car. I don't want him to see me until the very last minute, so I crawl in the backseat and wait for a Russell to emerge. My curiosity is killing me. I want to know what house he's in and with whom he is with.

I get out of the car and stare at the house in front of where he's parked. There is no one or nothing stirring about in the house. It's completely dark, so it's a longshot that he's in there. I walk down the block peering at each house closely, but nothing is calling my attention. This block is darker than the inside of a cave and quieter than a testing room. Maybe Russell only parked on this block, but is at a house a house on another block. Who the hell knows? I know I'm at my wit's end. Should I get back in Russell's car and wait or just get in my car and drive my ass home?

It's late and I'm in an unfamiliar neighborhood, so I think my best bet is to go home and settle things with Russell whenever he returns home. I won't even mention that I left the house. I'll just allow him to tell his side of the story of where he's been and then catch him in his lies. As I walk back to my car, I can't help but to look at every house and wonder if Russell is inside of it. I wish I could just walk into each one of these homes to see who is inside, but obviously, I can't. I'll just have to settle for catching Russell in his lies.

I make it to my car and start it up. I set my GPS to my home address and proceed to pull out of the parking space I'm in. While I'm pulling out, I'm elated at what I see. I immediately pull back into the parking space. How could I have missed something that was right in my face? I guess I was in such a rush to get to Russell's car that I totally disregarded it. My headlights shined on the door of a house that has a monogrammed silver door plate. Talk about being in the right place at the right time. To my surprise, the initials on the silver monogrammed plate read exactly as Cassie Monroe's would read.

Talk about some conniving bastards. They're going behind my back and sleeping together. I really didn't see this coming, but it's here and I'm forced to deal with it. I get out of my car and walk to the front of her house. There are no lights on and is pitch black. The absence of lights and movement doesn't deter me because I know this is Cassie's house and I know Gem's in there. There is no way in hell that this is a coincidence. I climb the gate in front of her house and walk up the stairs of her porch. I look inside her window, but can't see anything. Next, I bang on her door thunderously and ring the doorbell madly. Unfortunately, no one answers the door. After that, I walk around the side of the house to see if I can see something more incriminating than just Russell's car being on Cassie's block. As I tread slowly and quietly, I hear romantic music playing. My blood begins to boil with anger. As I get closer, I hear what sounds like water splashing and a woman moaning. I know I've heard that moan before. That's definitely Cassie moaning.

"Fuck me harder! Russell, fuck me harder damn it!" Cassie says.

My fears are confirmed in this moment. I can't hold back my tears this time. I don't know what to do. I walk to the backyard, but remain hidden. Cassie and Russell are in a jacuzzi she has in her backyard on the patio. Cassie is bent over the edge of the jacuzzi and Russell is fucking her from the back. I freeze momentarily as I look in disbelief. It's one thing to think your man is cheating, but there is no preparation for actually seeing it with your eyes.

I've seen all I need to see for the night. I'm getting my ass out of here. I can't take any more of this. I take a few steps to exit the backyard and then I hear Russell speaking.

Russell voices, "Cassie, this is the best pussy I've ever had.

"Is it really that good, baby? Is it better than Kim's?" Cassie asks.

Russell answers, "This pussy is better than I can explain. And yes, it's better than Kim's. Ya pussy is wetter and tighter than hers. Hands down."

Russell is out his damn mind! How dare he tell her that? I can't believe he said that. See, they've fucked with the wrong one tonight! Actually, they've fucked with the right one tonight. I got something for them. I pop out from my hiding spot and make myself known. Russell and Cassie both look at me with a look of confusion and shock. Russell dismounts Cassie.

"Kim, I know this looks bad, but it's not what you're thinking it is," Russell blurts out.

I say, "Russell shut the fuck up! You're right, it's not what I'm thinking. It's what I know. I'm not even gonna get mad at your trifling asses."

Cassie chimes in, "Kim, give us a minute to explain. It'll all make sense if you hear us out."

"Bitch bye! It all makes sense now. I heard Russell tell you that your pussy is better than mine. That's all I needed to hear!" I shout madly.

Kim and Russell both attempt to get out of the bubbling jacuzzi water. They seemed to be enjoying the jacuzzi tremendously, so I figure they can continue enjoying it forever. I quickly grab the patio lamp and throw it in the water. Cassie and Russell convulse profusely as the electric current electrocutes them. Seconds later, their bodies fall lifelessly into the jacuzzi. I run out of the backyard to my car and drive home. I make it home without being detected by anyone. I quickly strip my clothes off and take a shower. I laugh devilishly at how their bodies went into shock as the electric current overtook them. I finish showering and go to bed.

"Kim! Kim! Wake up. It's time for you to get up or you'll be late for your appointment," Russell states as he shakes me.

"Russell? What the hell is going on?" I ask confusedly.

"You were about to be late for your appointment. Get up!" Gem replies.

"What? Are you saying I was asleep?" I inquire.

"Yes, you were knocked out, but it's time to get up!" Gem verbalizes urgently.

I answer, "I just had a crazy ass dream, but it seemed so real. Oh my goodness, it was like the most vivid dream I've ever had."

Gem answers, "Well, you're gonna have to tell me about it later, but for now you have to get up and get ready."

"Okay, I'm up. I'll be ready in no time," I respond.

CHAPTER 7

A few days have gone by since the blowup with Cassie. Fortunately, we haven't heard from or seen her since then. I guess that little riff we had was enough for her to get the message. Gem hasn't even mentioned her and has put the incident behind him. I'm happy that he isn't dwelling on it because it could impact his writing negatively. The last thing we need is for his writing to cease or slow down because of that threesome. I would feel extremely terrible if it did because I'm to blame. I'm the one who setup the threesome to begin with. I'm guilty of inviting tumult into a once tranquil relationship.

Gem doesn't feel like cooking breakfast this morning and neither do I. For this reason, we are headed to the Corner Store Bakery for breakfast. I've never had it before, but I've only heard fantastic things about it. I hope it's as good as it's hyped up to be. Unfortunately, many times when people rave about how good something is, it turns out not to match the praise it received. Gem's driving as he does most of the time. I rarely drive when he's in the car with me.

The drive isn't very far from where we live as it pertains to distance, but the traffic sometimes makes it longer than it should be. Fortunately, we make it to the eatery with no trouble. Gem exits the car and walks around my side to open the door for me. Gem and I walk toward the restaurant. In most instances, I'm always freezing while in restaurants, so I tell Gem to reach in the backseat of the car and retrieve my jacket. Being the gentleman that he is, he does so.

We enter the establishment and walk to the counter. The place smells delicious. Gem and I both hope that the pleasant aroma is indicative of the taste of the food. If it is, we'll be overly satisfied. We peruse the menu and then make a selection. After we order, Gem and I find a seat. I have a thing for window seats, so we sit in a booth that has a perfect view of the street. People watching has always been my thing.

I tell Gem about some ideas I have for us to go on vacation. We always take an epic getaway each year. A few minutes later, the waitress brings us our food. I'm so ready to kill this deliciously smelling food. As we eat, I look out the window and suddenly I lose my appetite. My appetite is stolen from me, not because the food isn't delicious, but for a more troubling reason. I become frozen in my seat. I don't know if fear has overtaken me or if it's rage, but whatever the cause, I'm paralyzed. Gem notices my sudden pause and is staring at me in bewilderment.

"Is something wrong with you?" Gem inquires.

"Yes, it is! Don't be obvious, but look at the door of the restaurant. You're not going to believe your eyes," I tell.

"You have to be fucking kidding me! Not again," Gem blurts out as he sees Cassie Monroe walking into the Corner Store Bakery with a lady we don't know.

I don't know what we should do. I don't know if we should approach them or act like we don't see them. We now know for sure that there is no way that this isn't premeditated. Cassie probably has the other woman with her to make it seem like she's not up to anything. After staring for a moment, Gem looks away from them and resumes eating his breakfast. I don't want to continue eating, but I follow Gem's lead and continue to eat as well. Gem and I get back to conversing about business. We decide to not give Cassie any more of our attention even though we're bewildered as to how she found out where we were again.

Gem and I finish eating and are ready to depart. I have to use the ladies' room, so I head that way. Unfortunately, Cassie and her friend are sitting at a booth that I have to walk past in order to get to it. I really have to use the restroom and have no choice, but to walk past her table. I'm not risking destroying my bladder just to avoid Cassie. I'm not afraid of her. I walk by their table and Cassie stares at me. If looks could kill, I'd be six feet under already.

I make it to the bathroom with nothing more than a stare from Cassie. I'm using the restroom, when I hear what I think is Gem shouting. I also hear a female's voice shouting that I believe is Cassie's voice. I rush my bodily function, quickly wash my hands, and run to the bathroom door. When I fling the door open, my thoughts are confirmed. Gem's blocking the door and Cassie is yelling at him.

"Gem, what's going on out here? What the hell happened that you two are out here arguing?" I inquire frantically.

"Nothing major," Gem answers. "Let's go!"

"I'm not going anywhere until somebody tells me what is going on! I was only in the bathroom for two minutes and now it's drama," I say frankly.

Cassie speaks, "I don't know what your man's problem is. I came to use the bathroom and all of a sudden, he runs and cuts me off from entering like he owns the damn place. Last time I checked, I can use the bathroom whenever the hell I want!"

"I'm just making sure you don't try to hurt my

wife with your crazy ass! If blocking the door kept her safe, then I did my job. Fuck all the other shit," Gem responds.

"Oh, your ass was trying to jump me in the bathroom! You did the right thing baby," I speak.

"Wasn't nobody trying to jump you in the bathroom! I see why you two are together. You both are crazy as hell! I'm just trying to use the bathroom," Cassie reports.

I go to curse Cassie out, but I'm interrupted by the restaurant manager. She walks over to us in the bathroom corridor to investigate what's going on. Gem tells the manager that the situation is resolved and apologizes for disturbing the restaurant and its customers. He grabs me by the hand and we exit expeditiously. Gem isn't one for public disturbances, so it isn't surprising to me that we exited as quickly as we did. We head straight to the car and pull off. Gem and I are both irate about the incident with Cassie. I'm more upset about it because I had accepted the fact that the drama was over. It's a huge letdown knowing that it's still alive and well.

We arrive home and Gem makes some phone calls. He calls his lawyer to find out what options we have for dealing with Cassie and her stalking. He considered calling the police, but we eventually decided against that. The reason we went against calling the cops is because that could turn into a public relations nightmare. We would have to tell the cops all of the details of how we met Cassie. We really don't want those details released if they don't have to be.

Gem and his lawyer talk for about forty-five minutes about the Cassie situation. It turns out that we made the right decision by calling Gem's lawyer first. He informs Gem that Cassie hasn't done anything to us that would warrant the police to take action. The only thing we would've done by going to the authorities was waste our time. He further tells Gem that Cassie needs to do something more egregious for it to be a criminal offense.

Gem and his lawyer finish discussing the matter at hand and end the call. Gem is extremely concerned about how Cassie is able to show up everywhere we go. He's certain she's not following us because we've never noticed her car tailing us and we've been keeping our eyes wide open. Gem tells me to walk outside with him because he wants to check something.

Gem says, "Look around the car and see if you see something."

"Okay Babe, but something like what?" I ask.

He answers, "Something that doesn't belong. I'm wondering if she put some type of tracking device on our car, so she could know where we we're going without having to follow us through traffic. She wouldn't have to risk losing us or us seeing her following us. It could be small or big."

"Well damn! Now, it's definitely not that

serious. All of this is just too much," I reply.

"I know it is, but look. I can't think of any other way she's getting to us. Unless she put something in one of our phones without us knowing," Gem voices.

"I guess that could be it. The only things that are always where we are or in the vicinity are our phones and cars. I'm not getting on the ground to look though. You can get all dirty down there. I'll check the high ground," I remark.

Gem stoops down low and reaches around the bottom of the car, but doesn't feel anything. I look on the top of the car to see if there is anything amiss, but I don't have any luck either. Next, I go over to Gem's car and begin searching, but I don't spot anything on the outside. Gem tells me to check the inside of the cars for anything. I do as he says, but I don't find a thing. Gem decides to get down on the ground and look under the car more meticulously. After a few minutes of checking, Gem yells out.

"Son of a bitch! I fucking knew it!" he yells excitedly.

"What Babe? You found something?" I inquire.

Gem stands up and has a small circular device with what looks like a beacon light on it. Whatever it is surely does look like a tracker. It's not very high-tech, but it obviously works. Gem runs over to his car and checks under it. Again, he finds a device that's identical to the one he found under my car. He's both livid and satisfied. He's satisfied because he was able to find the hidden devices and livid because Cassie had the gumption to do something like this. I'm just dumbfounded at how far this person is willing to go to get what she wants. Gem immediately smashes both of the tracking devices.

"Now, we don't have to worry about her popping up on us anymore! That bitch is ludicrous! I'm gonna call my lawyer back and tell him what we found. Let's go back inside," Gem comments.

"Listen, you go back inside and call your attorney. I'm gonna run to the store. We have nothing in here for dinner and I have to make a quick stop at the printing company," I state.

Gem speaks, "Now you know that crazy ass Cassie is on the prowl. You need to stay here or I'll go with you. Just give me a minute."

"It's totally unnecessary. You already found the trackers, so she'll have no idea where I am. I'm only going to be gone for a short while," I convey.

"I hear what you're saying, but I'm coming with you. You can either stay home altogether or we're going together. Take your pick," Gem states bluntly.

"Well, I have to go to the printing company, so I guess we're going together. I'm ready when you are," I vocalize.

We both go back inside the house to get what

we need to depart. Gem calls his attorney on the way to the printing company, but he doesn't answer. We arrive at our destination and walk inside. We have to look at some samples for some promotional materials. Gem and I normally don't agree right away, but today is different; we're in complete agreement with which flyers and posters are best.

We leave the printing company and go to the grocery store. As we're parking the car, Gem's lawyer returns Gem's call. The grocery store is always loud, so Gem stays in the car. He knows that I'll be safe in a heavily populated grocery store even if Cassie manages to show up somehow. I get out of the car and head inside. I'm only getting a few items for dinner and won't be in the store for very long. To my delight, the store isn't very packed. I cruise down the few aisles that I need to go to.

As I turn down the aisle to get broccoli, I see Cassie heading straight toward me. I'm not afraid of her, so I stand my ground. She has quite an ominous look on her face and so do I. Cassie attempts to walk up to me and get in my face, but I prevent her from doing so. I put my shopping cart between her and me.

Cassie inquires, "What's your fucking problem?"

"I don't have a fucking problem! Listen, I'm not doing this in this aisle for all to see. If you want to talk, there's a restroom in the back corner," I communicate.

"Lead the way," Cassie speaks.

"How did you know I was at the grocery store?" I inquire in a puzzled tone.

"I followed you and Gem in my friend's car because we need to talk," Cassie answers angrily.

We make it to the restroom. Luckily for us, it's empty. We lock the door, so we can speak without interruption. Cassie is very emotional to say the least. I'm an emotional wreck as well. It's only right that we're emotional because it's been very chaotic since we met at In the Mix. We begin to converse.

"What do you need to talk to me about so urgently?" I ask.

"I need to know why you keep showing up to all of the places I'm at. This really needs to stop before I get the authorities involved," Cassie speaks sharply.

I respond, "You know why! I don't know why you're acting the way you are. I need you to bring the sweet and caring Cassie back. I haven't done anything to warrant the police being called anyway."

"You're a stalker! You dumb bitch! You've popped up at every promotional event I've had over the last three months and you weren't invited. I can't even go to breakfast or for a jog without you being there. I haven't been sweet to you. I'm a businesswoman; it's my job to be friendly with people and make connections.

You're in business too, so you should know that!" Cassie informs angrily.

"I'm not a stalker and I resent you saying that. You can call the authorities if you want, but they won't do anything. Like you said, I'm in business too, so I have a justified reason to be at the same events you're at. They'll laugh in your face if you make any allegations. Listen, I know your job is to make connections and we made one hell of a connection on the night of Gem's birthday party. I think we should keep that going," I voice.

Cassie responds, "That's the angle you're going to play! You'll just make it seem like it's merely a coincidence that you've been everywhere I've been lately. You really are one sick bitch! As far as the threesome that night, it was just something fun to do. It wasn't for keeps, it was for kicks. We fulfilled our wildest fantasies that night."

"Yes, that's the angle I'm going to play because that's what it is... sheer coincidence. I sell books and you sell magazines, so it's only sensible that our paths cross from time to time. I would appreciate it if you would stop calling me names. I agree that the night of passion we had was fun, but there was something more than just fun that happened that night," I word.

"What are you talking about? What else happened that night outside of a late-night alcohol induced tryst?" Cassie inquires.

I answer, "First of all, the night we met was predestined! All of the stars and planets aligned that night and that's why we met. Then, you and I hit it off while at In the Mix that night. We're both driven and have plenty of things in common. Lastly, the way you kissed and touched me at the hotel that night was like no other."

Cassie chimes in, "Girl, I don't know a damn thing about the stars and planets aligning. This is some crazy shit you're talking about! I'm really at a loss for words. It was sex... A fun night... A fuck! That's all it was!"

"I know you have to be kidding me. The way you kissed and touched me was magical. You can't fake intimacy like that. Our bodies were one that night and you can't deny it. When you were eating me out I wanted to cry because it felt so good. When I released, I felt my soul leave my body and connect with yours. We became one that night," I explain as I go to rub Cassie's hand.

Cassie pulls her hand away and states, "For the last time, it wasn't anything other than a fuck. I'm glad you enjoyed the night we had and so did I. I'll never forget it. Russell was even more amazing than I thought he'd be, but that's your husband and you two have a special thing going and I won't intrude again."

"You don't have to be so cold to me, Cassie. The truth is that I love you. Don't be mad at me. Please don't," I beg.

"I'm not trying to be mean to you. You're a sweet woman, but you need to direct your love to Russell. Again, I'm not the type of person to break up a happy home," Cassie articulates.

"Who says that someone should only love one person?" I inquire.

"My goodness! I'm not even answering that. You're not hearing me. This conversation is pointless! You're doing way too much. You've had me baffled for a quite a while. I couldn't figure out how you always managed to show up to where I was going, but when I discovered my monthly planner was missing, I figured you had to have it. I thought back and it went missing the same day you and I met to discuss Gem's interview for the magazine," Cassie voices.

"Yes, that's right, but I had to take it. It was the only way I got to see you. You're always so busy and wouldn't return my calls," I utter softly. "Look what I had to do to get us together for a second time... I had to pull a lot of strings to get Gem booked at the book festival in South Carolina."

"You have a husband! And whatever strings you pulled weren't for us!" Cassie yells as she pushes past me to exit the restroom.

I reply as I block the door, "I did do it for us. I even slipped a mickey in Gem's drink that night at the hotel in Columbia, so he'd be unconscious and we could have each other without him."

"Whatever!" Cassie blurts out. "Bitch you are cray-cray!"

Cassie leaves and doesn't say anything else. I'm dumbfounded by how nonchalant she is about how we connected that night. I read her eyes and body language that night and could tell we were in sync with one another. She even said that she'd never forget it, so it has to be something there. Why else would she not forget it? She can't just come into my life and make such a huge impact and just leave like that. She must be out of her damn mind!

CHAPTER 8

Okay, so I clearly misinterpreted the way that Cassie feels about me. Sometimes things go that way, but I get it now. I know what I have to do. I have to make things right. I hope that I haven't damaged Russell's relationship with Cassie. His career can really be boosted by Cassie's magazine. Russell being on the cover of the magazine and having an exclusive interview with Cassie will be invaluable to his writing career. Once his face graces the cover of *Black People Magazine*, his sales will go through the roof. I hope it's not too late to set this straight.

I haven't talked to Cassie in a week since the altercation in the restroom. Not that I haven't tried to reach her because I have. I've called her a couple of times and left a voice message as well as texted her. Cassie has distanced herself from me and I don't blame her because I would have done the same thing if someone was pursuing me with unwanted advances. I'm confident that we'll do business in the future because the conflict we had was all one big misunderstanding. Also, there is too much at stake for this drama not to be resolved. Cassie is a business woman at the end of the day and she knows that her readers would love to see Russell on the cover of her magazine. Russell is smoking hot within the female African American community, so her sales will surely spike. Russell joins me in the kitchen.

"Hey, Babe," I greet warmly.

Russell kisses me on the forehead and speaks, "Good afternoon Baby."

"Listen, I need to run something past you," I word in a concerned voice.

"It must be huge if you prefaced it like that. Of course, I'm all ears," Russell replies.

"Okay, so you know that Cassie and I aren't on the best of terms to say the least. That's not a good thing because our sour relationship is going to hurt your writing career. I have to fix it otherwise you'll never make the cover of her magazine and you damn sure won't get the interview," I orate.

"That goes without saying. Her audience is our target audience for the books. That's why it was such a match made in heaven when we linked up. That part of our company is your specialty, so fix it. Make it happen," Russell states frankly.

"Right! I know I need to fix it and you're right

about it being my responsibility, but I don't quite know how to fix it. She won't take my calls or respond to my texts," I voice in a hopeless tone.

"Well, have you been to her office?" Russell asks.

"Uh, no! You know I can't go down there. She'll probably call the cops on me if I show up down there. I'm not trying to go to jail. That would really hurt the company," I answer.

"So, are you telling me that you want me to go down there to talk to her?" Russell inquires.

"No, I'm not saying that either," I respond.

"Kim, you're giving me a headache. You don't want to go to her office yourself, but you don't want me to go, but you want to make things right. This is too much back and forth," Russell speaks.

I comment, "I know that I'm all over the place... I apologize. I guess I'm just looking for a little direction."

"Okay, here's my best advice. I'll say my part and let you decide what you want to do, but you have to own it. You said a moment ago that you want to fix it, so I think you should. I remember when we first started our company and you were apprehensive about doing so, but you quit your job and went full throttle for the company and looked how it turned out. You need to face this situation with the same fierceness that you did years ago. I remember how accomplished you felt when it all worked in our favor. I think you'll feel a lot better about things if you take control of this," Russell narrates. "Don't forget that I always have your back, so I'll do whatever you need me to do."

"Thanks, Russell. I get it now. I'll make it happen!" I convey confidently.

Russell tells me that he knows I will and leaves the kitchen. I just have to appeal to her on a business level to get this done. Hell, we're both very polished business women, so she'll have to understand where I'm coming from. I know she's not answering my calls, so I'll have to take it a step further. Russell basically told me to be aggressive and go to her office, so I'm going to do just that. You can't be passive in anything you do in life. Chances are, if you take the passive approach, you won't be successful.

I go upstairs and get cleaned up. An hour later, I have on my fiercest business suit. This is my "I mean business" suit. It's an all-black skirt with the matching jacket and white-collared shirt. I have my hair pulled straight back in a ponytail without a strand of hair out of place. I've closed countless deals for Russell in this outfit and today will not be any different. I'm going to pop up at her office and I won't take no for an answer.

I throw on my black red bottom pumps and head for the car. Twenty minutes later, I arrive at Cassie's office and walk in. Her secretary looks at me with a weird look as soon as she sees me. She obviously knows that Cassie and I are on bad terms and is wondering what I'm doing here. She picks up the phone and makes a call as I make it to her desk. I wait patiently for her to get off the phone.

The secretary hangs up the phone and asks, "Can I help you?"

"Yes, I'm Kim Davenport and I'm here to speak with Cassie Monroe," I answer.

"I don't see that you have an appointment," she says as she appears to peruse the appointment book.

I know she didn't really have to look at the appointment book to know that because she knows who I am. I'm no fool, but I guess she wants to remain professional. Seconds later, Cassie emerges from the direction of her office with two security officers. Cassie and the security guards are all heading in my direction. I'm not the least bit surprised. I'm just glad that she's with them. I speak as they walk toward me. I have a small skit to play out. As they approach, I pull a white handkerchief out of my handbag. I wave it in the air over my head and then throw it to the floor. Cassie and the guards stop before me.

"Before you throw me out, I just want to apologize. I threw the white handkerchief as an offer of peace and my sincerest apology. I'm sorry for the ruckus I've caused and it won't happen again. I just need five minutes of your time. Please indulge me, but if you don't, I'll understand," I vocalize humbly.

Cassie's guards look at her to see what she wants to do. She motions for them to let me speak without them throwing me out. I know I have a chance to set things right now. I tell Cassie thanks for letting me speak. However, she doesn't respond verbally. Instead, she taps her watch as to say that the clock is ticking. Next, she leans slightly to her left and folds her arms. The floor is all mine!

I talk quicker than ever before, "Again, I'm sorry for everything. We have an opportunity for both of us to benefit financially with Russell being on the cover of your magazine. We'll serve our audiences simultaneously, so it's only right that we get this done. Business doesn't have to suffer because of personal matters. Lastly, I'll be completely silent on this. You can deal exclusively with Russell and won't have to see me ever again. Please don't penalize Russell because of me. I'm done."

Cassie collects her thoughts for a moment before she speaks, "Hmm, You're right. My audience would love to see Russell on the cover and hear his story. I don't think they should suffer because of nonbusiness-related affairs. If I do it, it'll be completely on my terms and you can't be involved in the photo shoot or the interview."

"Whatever you say, we'll do! I promise. This is all business. No emotions involved," I voice.

"Okay, I'm in, but I replaced all the meetings

that I had scheduled with you and Russell with other clients, so Russell will be rescheduled during some awkward times, but I don't think the photo shoot will be too hard to reschedule. Nonetheless, I'll have my secretary contact Russell, so be sure that he's awaiting my office to contact him," Cassie says sternly.

Cassie walks back to her office and her security guards escort me off of the premises. She didn't speak a word of goodbye or thank you before she walked off, but I'm fine with that. I came here with an agenda and I met it. That's all that matters to me. I'm sure that Russell will be just as excited as I am. He was right about me taking control of the situation. We all know that scared money doesn't make money. I decide to wait until I get home to tell Russell the good news. I want to see the excitement in his eyes as I tell him how I wheeled and dealed to get him the cover and interview back.

A while later, I make it home to share the great news to Russell. Russell walks into the living room as I'm entering the house. He looks at me and I look away. When I look away, Russell automatically thinks that I didn't get the deal done. I purposely mislead him because I love a good joke. Russell hugs me and rubs my back to console me. I fall comfortably into his embrace.

"It's alright Kim. There will be other magazines that are going to leap to do business with us. This one wasn't for us. We're to blame for not landing the cover with Cassie's magazine anyway," Russell articulates.

"I agree with you on that. There will be others, but I don't agree with you when you say that we're to blame for not landing this one," I comment.

"How could you not agree? You know we had the magazine locked in before the threesome right? You don't think that mixing business with pleasure was poor decision making on our part?" Russell asks.

"Well, in most cases yeah, but seeing as how I got us the magazine cover and interview back on the table, I don't see how the two correlate!" I convey proudly and enthusiastically.

Russell speaks jokingly, "Oh, you played me! That's so cold!"

He reaches down to the couch and grabs a pillow. When he reaches for the pillow, I take off running. Russell takes off after me to hit me with the pillow for playing with his emotions. I run into the foyer and Russell catches up to me. He gently hits me with the pillow as I laugh at him and block the pillow's blows. I manage to grab the pillow out of his hands and then he takes off running. Unfortunately, he's too fast for me to catch him, so I throw the pillow at him while he's running away. My thrust is accurate and bops him upside his head. We both crack up laughing.

We're both happy because we know that him being on the cover of the magazine pretty much ensures that he's going to have another best seller. I walk over to Russell and he gives me a fist bump. I fill him in on the details of how I stole the deal back for us. He tells me that he's proud of me and that he knew I could do it.

"So, when do we have to meet with her and her team?" Russell asks.

"Well, that's the catch. I won't be meeting with Cassie or any of her team on this one. It'll be all you. Those are the terms of the agreement," I communicate.

"Damn, I don't know about that Babe. I mean, we're a team and we do everything together. My lady, this is our thing, so if Cassie doesn't accept you, then she doesn't accept me," Russell voices.

"Honey, thank you, but it's not that serious. This is business and not the time for a moral stance to be made. It's better this way because we'll still get the deal done. We made a mistake by mixing business with pleasure and still are going to benefit from it. We just have to treat this as a learning experience and never do it again. The cover and interview are a go! I'll be fine with not being involved," I explain.

"I feel you on that. It's your call. If you like it, I love it. Honey, I just want you to know that I'd never choose money over you," Russell tells. "Babe, the night I proposed to you under the stars and moonlight on the beach in Barbados with the waves splashing us, I told you that you are my world and I meant it and it still applies today."

"Well, I love it, so we're going to go forward with it. Russell, I know that you would choose me. Also, it's not like I'm not going to be involved anyway. I'll coach you up on what to do from behind the scenes," I reply. "Oh yeah, we're also on standby as far as the meeting time is concerned, so we'll just start prepping immediately."

"You're the boss on this aspect of the company, so your wish is my command," Russell shoots back.

I remark sarcastically, "Damn right I am and you better not forget it!"

Russell and I spend the night going over some potential questions he'll be asked during the interview. In addition to that, we look through a bunch of head shots we have of Russell just in case we have to use one of them instead of using Cassie's photographer.

CHAPTER 9

It's been a week since I went to Cassie's office unannounced and secured Russell's interview and magazine cover for *Black People Magazine*. Things weren't looking good on it actually happening because it took Cassie's office several days to call Russell with a time and place for the interview. Russell started thinking they'd never call him back, but I wasn't concerned. Cassie has always been a woman of her word, so I figured it would just be a matter of time for her or her office to reach out. I think she was probably waiting to see if I'd contact her first then she'd call everything off because that would have been a violation of the terms of our agreement.

Fortunately, Cassie's office called earlier today to tell Russell that he needs to meet Cassie at Sensations Coffee Shop. Russell and I are both excited about the future. The delay in hearing from Cassie's office played right into our favor because that gave me ample time to prepare for their meeting. Everything is planned out for this all the way from what Russell is going to wear, down to what he's going to say and do. Honestly, I wish I could go with him, but I can't. I'll just have to read it in the magazine at some point.

Russell is getting dressed for the meeting. I'm sure he's looking handsome as ever in his blue business suit. He was a little upset about the time of the meeting because he had plans for tonight and really didn't expect to have an evening meeting for the interview. We've always operated on a business before pleasure principle, so Russell had no choice other than to cancel his plans for tonight. He's on his way downstairs now.

"Well, you look dapper as always!" I speak as I stand at the foot of the steps.

"I am who I am! Looking good is what I do!" Russell replies confidently.

"Boy bye! You know your head stays in the clouds, but you do look handsome though," I comment as he hugs me.

"Thanks. Well, let me get rolling. You know I'd rather be early than be late," Russell voices.

He's always the type to be early. Being late is one of his biggest pet peeves and he considers tardiness to be highly unprofessional. On too many occasions to count, Russell has had us extremely early to events we were hosting or attending. To my dismay, we've even showed up to venues in the past before they actually opened. He can do that tonight by himself if his heart desires.

"I know you loathe being late Mr. Early Bird! Seriously, good luck even though I know you'll be fine. If for some reason you get stuck during the interview, call or text me. I'll be waiting by the phone," I convey, as I adjust his collar and smooth out his jacket.

"I'll be fine. Now, you might be the one who needs some assistance. You know you're a nervous wreck when you're not in control," Russell remarks.

"No, I'm not. I'm normally fine. That's why I plan everything to the T. I don't like to worry, so I over plan. Thank you very much!" I state as I walk Russell to the car in the garage.

Russell says, "I'll see you later. Let me get outta here."

"Bye," I voice and give him a kiss through the open car window.

Russell backs out of the garage and heads to the coffee shop. Fifteen minutes after Russell leaves, I realize that he absent-mindedly left the headshots that he was supposed to give to Cassie for the magazine cover. Leave it up to a man to always forget something. I decide to take the photos to the coffee shop. I'll just put them in Russell's car, so he'll have them if he needs them. Besides, that's all I can do anyway. It's not like I can walk in the coffee shop and give them to

Cassie.

I head over to the coffee shop with pictures in hand. Ten minutes later, I arrive at the coffee shop. When I drive past, I see Cassie and Russell sitting in a booth by the window. I pull into a parking spot down the street from the coffee shop that allows me to observe what's going on. Fortunately, Russell looks relaxed and comfortable. Cassie appears to be very engaged in Russell's responses, but I'm not surprised because Russell is naturally very personable and I've prepared him thoroughly for this. I know how Cassie thinks because she's very similar in thought to me. If I didn't know any better, I'd think we were sisters or soul mates.

I hope Russell mentions growing up in a single parent home like I told him to. That story will really go over well with the magazine's followers because Russell was raised by his mom after his dad abandoned the family. The interview must be going better than expected because it was only slated to last an hour, but it hasn't ended yet. Now, Russell and Cassie are the only two customers still inside. Those book sales are going to skyrocket once this interview and photo hit the magazine. The timing couldn't be better.

I get out of the car to drop the photos in Russell's car. Unfortunately, as I make it to the car to drop the photos, Russell and Cassie come walking outside. I duck down behind Russell's car to hide. Russell, being the gentleman he is, walks Cassie to her car. She gets in and pulls out of the parking lot. As Russell approaches his car, I come out of hiding and reveal myself.

"Kim, what the hell are you doing out here?" Russell asks as he ensures that Cassie is out of sight.

"I wanted to give you this," I answer.

"What? Give me what? You know if Cassie would've seen you, this entire night would have been a waste?" Russell asks. "And why the hell are you dressed like that?"

I pull out a shiny, expensive, and very pointy letter opener and jab Russell through the throat with it. Blood squirts all over the black jacket and gloves that I'm wearing. Russell grabs his throat and falls to the ground as he shakes violently. Seconds later, he stops moving as the blood quickly exits his body. I snatch the envelope opener out of his throat. I take off the jacket and wrap the letter opener in it. I take the gloves off and throw them on Russell as his lifeless body lies on the ground. I walk back to the car and drive home.

During the drive home, I stash the bag and quickly get home. As soon as I get home I text Russell to see when he'll be home. I have to establish my alibi for when the authorities come. Next, I get in the shower to clean off. Of course, there is still no reply from Russell, but I'm sure by now someone has found Russell's body. I text Russell's phone again with a message that reads:

"I haven't heard back from you. Is everything alright?"

I wait twenty more minutes and then place a call to his phone. To my delight, someone engages the phone call. I knew it would only be a matter of time before someone noticed something and called the cops. It most likely was one of the coffee shop workers who made the call to the authorities. Either way, it's time to give the performance of a lifetime.

"Hi, honey. I was getting worried. You were taking a long time to respond," I say as the call engages.

"Ma'am, this isn't Russell Davenport. Who are you?" the person on the phone asks.

"Well, where is Russell? Who are you? And why are you answering his phone? Can you put Russell on the phone please?" I ask angrily.

"This is Homicide Detective Patrick Jones. Are you Mrs. Davenport?" he asks.

"Yes, this is Mrs. Davenport. Homicide? Where's my husband?" I ask urgently. "Did something happen to him?"

"Mrs. Davenport, I hate to tell you this, but your husband has been murdered," he answers.

I scream while pretending to cry, "No, no there must be some mistake. He was just here all well and fine. Tell me what happened!"

"Ma'am, I'm going to need you to identify the body and I'm gonna need you to come down to the station to answer a few questions," he replies.

"I'm sorry for your loss… I truly am."

I wail brokenly and ask, "What happened? Where did this happen? Are you kidding me? Somebody killed my husband? Answer what kind of questions?"

"Mrs. Davenport, I'm gonna send a unit to your house to bring you to the morgue and to the station and we'll answer as many questions as possible for you at that point," Detective Jones replies.

I've seen enough detective television shows to know that they always suspect the victim's spouse or significant other when someone is murdered. I'm well versed in what to do, so I'm not worried. I'm going to go into that police station and win an Oscar tonight. I get dressed in some clothes that don't match and are slightly wrinkled. I even have my hair slightly disheveled, but not over the top. I want to appear to be distraught, but I can't come off as over the top because they may see through my charade. Let's be clear; they already suspect me anyway, so I have to tread extremely carefully.

About twenty minutes later, an officer arrives at my home to take me to the morgue and police station. He's peering around my foyer in hopes of seeing something amiss, but he's not going to find anything. I grab my bag and we leave. Surprisingly, the officer doesn't say much to me or ask me any questions on the ride to the morgue. He wouldn't answer any of my questions either. I guess he's just a flunky and they don't trust him with this investigation. We arrive at the morgue and go inside. There are two men in here waiting. I assume one is the coroner from the way he's dressed and the other gentleman is an officer.

"Hello, Mrs. Davenport. I'm Detective Jones. I'm the one you spoke to on the phone earlier. I'm sorry that we have to meet under these circumstances," he communicates solemnly.

"I'm sorry as well," I reply while whimpering.

"This is Dr. Jackson. He's the coroner. Like I said on the phone, I wanted you to come down to identify your husband's body. This is often tough for many to do, but this is procedure and we have to do it," Detective Jones voices.

I nod my head in agreement with what he stated. I walk over to the table where a covered corpse rests. The coroner pulls back the sheet and Russell's dead body lies there. I have to decide how I want to play this. Should I dive on his dead body and scream? Should I fall into the detective's arms and weep? Should I just leave the room immediately? This is humorous to me on so many levels. Decisions, decisions, decisions. I stand frozen for a few seconds and allow a tear to trickle down my cheek without speaking.

"Ma'am, is this your husband's body?" asks Detective Jones.

"Yes, it's him" I answer as I turn and leave the

room.

I decide to play it cool and not scream and shout. I'm sure they've seen that routine a million times. I walk over to the water fountain in the hallway to take a drink of water. While I'm bent over drinking, I stick my finger down my throat and make myself throw up on the water fountain. I bet they haven't seen this one before. My timing is perfect because Detective Jones walks out of the room where Russell's body is just as I'm throwing up. He runs to my side to check on me.

"Mrs. Davenport, are you okay? Can I get you anything?" he asks while rubbing my back.

"No, I'm alright. I've just never seen a dead body before. I mean, I've been to funerals before, but I've never seen a dead body like that and to make matters worse it's my husband," I recite in a broken tone.

"I totally understand. I can't imagine what you're going through right now. I hate this part of the job with a passion. Being the bearer of bad news is never pleasant. Also, I hate that I have to ask you a series of questions down at the station. I hope you understand," he orates.

Yes, I understand. It's part of the job. I get it," I state frankly.

They escort me to the detective's car and we drive to the station. We walk inside and go immediately to an interview room. They bring me a box of tissue and a bottle of water. I hope they can't see how truly emotionless I am about this. I don't want to appear bored and unaffected, but I am. I really don't give a fuck about this. I just hate formalities. The detective offers me his condolences again and begins with his questioning.

"Did your husband have any enemies? Do you know of anyone who wished to cause your husband harm?" he asks.

I answer, "No, not that I know of. Russell appeared to have no enemies, but even if he did, he wouldn't share that information with me."

"Why do you say that ma'am? Was there any conflict in your marriage?" he inquires.

"Oh, no... no conflict. Russell just was the type of man who shielded me from things like that. He was my protector," I answer.

"I see. Well, we found him stabbed to death at the coffee shop on Middleton Street. Do you know why he was at the coffee shop to begin with?"

"Russell was an author and often wrote at what most people would call awkward times and places, so I figure he went there to write, but he didn't say explicitly where he was going or why. Our relationship was built on trust, so I never questioned his movements and he never questioned mine," I explain.

"I don't think he went there to write because we didn't find a laptop or any other typing device in his possession. Robbery clearly wasn't the motive because he was left with many valuables and cash was still in his wallet," he tells.

"I don't know what to say. I don't know of anyone who wanted to harm him," I utter.

"And ma'am where were you during the hours of let's say nine-thirty until right before you called you husband's phone?" he inquires.

"I was home all night waiting for Russell's return. I watched some television and took a shower. I wanted to be prepared for when Russell returned home. I never left," I verbalize.

"So, you didn't come to the coffee shop to meet your husband?" he asks.

"Sir, I just told you that I never left the house and I don't appreciate what you're implying," I say violently.

"Ma'am, I'm sorry if I offended you, but the clerk in the coffee shop said your husband met with a woman, but couldn't really describe her, so I had to ask. It's possible that whoever that woman is knows something about what happened. She may have been the last person to see him alive," Detective Jones clears up.

I convey, "I'm so sorry. I thought you were trying to imply that I had something to do with this. I totally misunderstood where you were going with that line of questioning."

"Mrs. Davenport, there's no need to apologize. I've been doing this for a very long time and I've had the worst of the worst said to me during questioning. It's all procedure," he voices.

We continue talking about Russell's death. The detective acts as if he believes me, but I know he's studying me closely. The interview is coming to an end, so we get up and walk into the hallway. He tells me that he'll be in touch with me if they get any new information and tells me to contact him if I think of anything that will help out. He gives me his business card as we walk outside the station. I get in the car with a cop who's going to drive me home. The drive back home is quieter than the initial ride to the morgue. I'm tired and don't want to talk too much because I may slip up. Hell, it's not every day that you kill your husband. A lot of patience, planning, and nerve went into this.

CHAPTER 10

I get home and go inside. I strip down and lie across my bed. Next, I contact Russell's family to tell them what happened. His family members are devastated by the unexpected news. After that, I log onto Russell's social media accounts and type statements about his senseless murder. Just like his family, his fans are also distraught. A few minutes later, my phone rings. Not surprisingly, the caller is Cassie Monroe. I figured she'd call once she saw what I posted. In fact, I really only posted the information about Russell to solicit her call.

"I saw what you posted to social media. Please, tell me that it's not true," Cassie says as I engage the call.

"Yes, it's very true. I wish it wasn't," I speak.

"What happened?" Cassie asks with concern.

"I don't feel like talking about it over the

phone. It's been a long night and I really don't feel like being alone right now," I articulate.

"I know we've had our differences, but I'm genuinely sorry for your loss. With that said, I'll stop by if you need someone to talk to," Cassie suggests.

"That would be nice. I'm really outta my mind right now," I vocalize.

"Text me your address. If you need anything, text me that too and I'll bring it through," Cassie words. "I'll be there shortly."

"Thanks girl. This means a lot to me," I state sincerely.

I get out of the bed and go to the kitchen. It may be a long night with Cassie, so I throw on a pot of coffee. I also chill some wine just in case she wants to sip an adult beverage. I'm slightly excited about seeing her. I can't help but to keep looking out the window waiting for her to arrive. I feel like a kid waiting for Christmas to arrive. I prepare myself to do some more acting before she gets here. Finally, I see her car pull into my driveway. I open the front door and stand on the porch. She gets out the car and walks up the stairs.

"Hey, girl," Cassie states as she comes through the door.

"Hey, thanks for coming," I say as we share a warm embrace.

Cassie replies, "Don't mention it. I can't imagine what you're going through."

"It's definitely tough. I'm filled with so many emotions right now that I almost can't control myself. It's like I'm enraged and sad at the same time. I'm in and out of different emotions right now," I convey as we sit on the couch.

"That's to be expected. And it's probably going to be like that for quite some time. Honestly, it's probably going to be like that forever. Anytime we experience a loss, especially an unexpected loss of this nature, we visit some very dark places emotionally," Cassie explains sympathetically.

"Yes, you couldn't be more correct. I'm sorry, where are my manners? Can I offer you some coffee, wine, or something else to drink?" I ask.

"Girl, you don't have to apologize right now. I know being cordial would be the furthest thing from my mind right now. Don't worry about that, but I could go for a glass of wine," Cassie comments.

I get up to fix the wine, but Cassie won't have it. She tells me to point her in the right direction and she'll fix the wine for us. I tell her it's in the kitchen and point her in that direction. With a sense of urgency, Cassie goes to the kitchen and returns with two glasses of wine. She sits next to me on the couch and rubs my leg as I lightly whimper. We sip the wine as we talk.

"I hope I'm not being too forward, but I am really interested to know what happened to Russell. I mean, it's hard to believe that he's dead because I was just with him. I'm at a loss for words right now," Cassie communicates.

I answer, "No, you're not being too forward. I totally understand your interest in the situation. I know what you mean because I was just with him too. Well, here's what happened. Russell was stabbed to death in the parking lot of a coffee shop at about 9:30 this evening."

"Oh my goodness! That's what time we left the coffee shop. That had to happen as soon as I pulled off from the coffee shop. I can't believe this. This is awful!!!" Cassie voices as she hugs me.

I'm really not hearing her words because her perfume is so enticing and I feel like I belong in her arms. I could stay here forever. I rest my head on her shoulder as she rubs my head and she tells me it's going to be alright eventually. I place a soft kiss on her neck and then I place a kiss on her lips. After the kiss on the lips, Cassie pulls away from me and stands up. She seems to be taken aback by my advance.

"I know you're going through a lot right now and I feel for your loss, but that's not what I'm here for. I'm here to console you at a time of grievance. No more, no less," Cassie articulates sternly.

"Cassie listen, I know you wanted to be with me, but couldn't because of Russell, but he's gone now. We don't have to worry about him anymore. We can love each other without any impediments," I remark.

"I never told you that I'd be with you if Russell was out of the picture. I never implied that or anything of the sort. I clearly told you that it was just some fun shit that we did. I don't know what the hell is wrong with you. You're crazy as hell!" Cassie narrates.

I reply, "I'm not crazy! I love you and I know you love me. You wouldn't be here if you didn't care about me. You got up out of your bed late at night because deep down inside you love me and want to be with me. Just admit it bitch!"

"Umm, on that note, I'm getting my ass out of here. I knew I shouldn't have brought my ass over here. I tried to be nice, even though my intuition, told me not to and look what it came to. Kim, goodbye! Again, I'm sorry for your loss, but don't contact me ever again," says Cassie angrily.

"I see how it is now! You made love to me and it meant nothing to you. You're just like these men out here fucking everything in sight with no strings attached," I utter.

"I'm done talking, girl bye," Cassie speaks. "Don't worry about the magazine interview either. That shit is a wrap!"

"Well, you better hope I don't decide to talk because the cops are surely interested in who Russell was with at the coffee shop. The clerk already told the authorities that he met with a woman, but they don't have a description of her,"

I communicate.

"Bitch, there's nothing to talk to the cops about, so do what you gotta do. In fact, fuck you. You don't have to do shit! I'll go talk to them my damn self. I know Russell was alive and well when I pulled out of that parking lot," blurts Cassie furiously as she walks to the door and attempts to open it.

I walk behind her and push the door closed and speak, "Hell, if that's what you want to do, then do it, but it may not go as smoothly as you think. Maybe you didn't do it, but there may be a lot of evidence out there making it look like you did it."

Cassie turns and faces me with a look of bewilderment and inquires, "What the hell are you talking about? What evidence would there be that I killed Russell?"

"Well, you were the last known person to see him alive, so that'll interest the cops. Next, I'm sure the police will be interested in why you texted and left voice messages for Russell a couple weeks back stating you two need to talk. It's gonna look like you two had a fling, but you wanted more and Russell didn't," I explain.

Cassie shoots back confidently, "I'm sure that a few messages won't lead to a conviction or even an indictment. I'm not the first person to text or call someone who has been murdered. It really seems like you're really trying to say I did this. I can see you're trying to set me up for this. Please unblock the door, so I can get away from your sick and twisted ass!"

I respond sinisterly, "I'm surprised by you right now. You're smart enough to surmise that I'm trying to set you up for this and you know I cover all bases, so you can't think a meeting and a couple of messages are all I have on you to take the fall for this. Shit, maybe I overestimated your level of perceptiveness. You can leave if you want to."

Not surprisingly, Cassie doesn't open the door to leave. I can tell that she's heavily considering leaving and taking her chances of going straight to the authorities and telling them she was with Russell at the coffee shop. I know her well enough to know that she's not going to do that without knowing what I have stacked against her. She's a woman who likes to be well-informed when she makes a decision, so she's not leaving until she has an idea of what I've concocted. She breathes deeply and walks over to the couch and sits down.

"Okay, I'll play your little game just for a second and I really do mean for a second because my patience is running thin with you," Cassie comments.

I voice arrogantly while snickering, "Cassie, that's cute, but you're not in control, so you can stop acting like you are. I'm not one of your office underlings because I'm running this shit right now, so shut the fuck up and listen bitch!"

"Oh, you tried it. You got me fucked up!" Cassie yells as she jumps up from her seat.

Her voice is strong and forceful. I can tell she's not afraid of me. The good thing is that I'm not afraid of her either and I have the upper hand. I'm holding all of the cards. I stand in front of her as she jumps up and push her back down to her seated position. She tries to get up again, but I slap her and pin her arms down.

"Stop moving and just listen. You'll see how precarious of a situation you are in," I state sternly as I look her eye ball to eye ball.

Fortunately, Cassie calmly nods her head and calms down. Her anger level is on ten right now. She's giving me the most evil look I've ever been given in my life. I'm not fazed by her death stares because they're empty. I sit down beside her, so we can speak.

"I don't want you to leave here thinking that you can go to the cops and tell your side of the story and everything be fine. I promise you, it will not. Even if I didn't have evidence that points to you being Russell's murderer, your company will be destroyed from the allegations. You'd lose all of your sponsorships for sure," I tell.

Cassie says, "Well, maybe I'll take my chances with the judicial system."

"Maybe a murder weapon that belongs to you will show up too. Maybe a bloody jacket that belongs to you will show up as well. Maybe evidence left at the scene that belongs to you will be linked to you through DNA. There is a lot of missing evidence connected to this case that may show up and convict you," I respond.

"You know I could strangle you right now? Why are you doing this? What do you want from me?" Cassie asks desperately.

"You stabbed Russell and now you want to strangle me?" I ask jokingly.

"That's not funny. I know this isn't about money because you and Russell were doing very well for yourselves," Cassie assures.

"Well, this is partly about money. You know that the magazine article and cover is going to send Russell's book sales through the roof, so you will go forward with that. Now, that he's dead, all of his material is going to fly off the shelves," I verbalize.

"Okay, consider it done. My team will have the article ready for our next edition, but we don't have a photo of him for the cover," Cassie states.

"Now, that's what I want to hear! You don't have to worry about the picture because I have plenty of headshots that would be great for your cover," I speak.

"That'll be fine. What's the other part of why you're doing this?" Cassie asks.

I answer, "It's about the way I feel about you. I want us to be together. We can build something very special if you're willing to give this love a try. I think it'll be sweet if we go on dates and make love like we did in the past, but if that doesn't work for you, you can just go to jail for the rest of your life. It's for you to decide."

"I see how it is. I guess we'll be spending some time together very soon, but at some point, I'll need whatever evidence you're blackmailing me with. It's only right," Cassie mentions.

"We'll cross that bridge when we come to it. For now, I look forward to us spending time together. I know this is forced, but I promise that I'll win your heart over," I communicate as I caress Cassie's face.

Cassie doesn't respond. She gets up and heads for the door again. I walk behind her as she does so. I tell her that I'll call her, so I can get her Russell's photo for the cover. She tells me that her office will be waiting for my call and she leaves. I clean up the wine glasses and get in the bed. Good times with Cassie are ahead.

CHAPTER 11

It's been a month since I murdered Russell at the coffee shop. The funeral was nice, but I didn't enjoy it because I had to pretend to be grief stricken the entire time. Outside of the funeral, the month has been a series of fortuitous happenings for me. The situation I'm most elated by is the relationship that Cassie and I have together. I either see or talk to her daily and when we make love, it's more magical and intense each time. We truly are two peas in a pod. I believe we are soul mates because Cassie finishes my sentences and I finish hers. Our like mindedness is unprecedented. We get along better than Russell and I did.

I'm proud to boast that Russell appeared on the cover of Cassie's magazine that released yesterday. He looks great on the cover and his interview is dazzling. I'm sure he's going to really cement his mark with his women fan base once they read it. The fact that Russell is dead has already caused a drastic spike in his sales and they'll only go up from here. My bank account is swelling more and more by the second. He'll gain thousands more followers once Cassie's readers get this edition of *Black People Magazine*.

Speaking of winning, I've even been cleared of having anything to do with Russell's murder. As always, the spouse is the number one suspect when their other half gets killed. Detective Patrick Jones questioned me several times about Russell's homicide trying to trip me up, but he never was able to make me falter. My story stayed the same every time I told it to him and his team. They even subpoenaed my cell phone records to see if my phone used cell towers near where the coffee shop is. I wasn't worried about that because I left my phone home for that reason. As I planned, they tested the gloves I wore when I killed Russell for DNA and were able to get a sample. Detective Jones asked me to provide a DNA sample to exclude me as a suspect and I obliged. The results of the test stated that my DNA didn't match the DNA that was in the gloves. I wasn't surprised because the gloves belonged to Cassie. I wore latex gloves over my hands, so I wouldn't leave my DNA. However, Cassie's DNA is definitely on those gloves.

Once the officers cleared me of any

wrongdoing as it pertains to Russell's murder, I was able to collect on Russell's handsome insurance policy. He wanted to make sure if anything ever happened to him I would be set for life. He was successful in his endeavor because I'm set. His policy even had a provision for the house to be paid off upon his death. All is well in the world right now. Cassie is even making dinner for me right now.

Cassie shouts upstairs, "Girl, are you ready to eat?"

"Baby, I'm ready to eat dinner and you!" I shoot back.

"Just a freak is what you are. Well, dinner is ready. You can eat that first and then you can taste that other thing for dessert," Cassie remarks.

Cassie and I enjoy a delicious chicken parmesan meal as we sip wine and listen to music. After we finish eating, we slow dance in the living room. I love this woman to death. I never imagined that I'd love someone more than I did Russell, but I do. We dance, kiss, and grope one another for several songs. I am hot and bothered right now and need to release immediately, so I lead Cassie upstairs to my bedroom. Cassie pushes me down on my bed and strips me of all my clothes.

"You said you wanted something else to eat?" Cassie asks.

"Yes, I did say I wanted to devour something for dessert and I'm looking right at it. I hope you give me more than I can handle," I retort.

"It's so much to eat that it's never gonna run out. You're gonna get what you asked for; I promise you that. You're gonna fuck around and drown from eating my pussy," Cassie tells me as she licks on my nipples.

"I like the sound of that! If you get that wet, that means I gave you what you came for!" I reply.

"Honey, I know that's right! I'm trying to get kinky tonight. It's only right because you've been a bad girl lately," Cassie says.

I inquire as I nuzzle Cassie's neck, "Kinky? Kinky how?"

"I can show you better than I can tell you," Cassie voices.

She rises from off of my body and goes to her overnight bag and emerges with four silk scarves. She comes back over to the bed and sensually caresses my body with them. The silk is very smooth on my skin. Cassie grabs my foot and ties one of the scarves around my ankle and then ties the other end of the scarf to my footboard bedpost. She dances around the room gyrating and rubbing her body as she ties my other foot and both arms to the three remaining bedposts.

Cassie is sexually domineering and I love it. I've never been tied up before, so I'm very intrigued as to what she'll do to me. I hope she sits on my face as she said she would. I want to eat her pussy to the point that she reaches new levels of ecstasy. My walls are becoming inundated with moisture just fantasizing about it. She climbs on top of me and straddles me. Her body is perfect and she is the epitome of sexy. She kisses me and then faintly bites my bottom lip. She knows exactly what I like.

Cassie wraps her hands around my throat and gently squeezes. The pressure she's applying for choking me is perfect. It's the perfect amount of force to turn me on. She knows my body so well. It feels like her hands were made to touch my body. Seconds later, I feel her grip around my neck getting tighter and tighter to the point where it's getting uncomfortable. Unfortunately, she's not loosening her grip and is applying more pressure to my neck.

"You're hurting me," I say in a garbled tone. "I can't breathe."

When she doesn't lighten up, I repeat it again, but that doesn't help my situation. Next, I begin to shake violently in an attempt to break free from her clutch, but it too is to no avail. Shit, I'm trapped with no way to escape. I feel myself getting eerily close to becoming unconscious, but I refuse to die like this. I keep squirming and making as much noise as I can muster and Cassie finally let's go.

She gets off the bed and exits the room. I can hear her running down the stairs. I use all of my might to escape the perilous predicament that I'm in, but it's useless. My arms and legs are wrapped tightly and there is no wiggle room to escape. What the fuck can I do? My only recourse is to scream at the top of my lungs in hopes of someone hearing me. I know the chance of someone hearing me is slim, but I have to do what I can.

I'm screaming at the top of my vocal ability and I hear Cassie running back up the steps. She appears in the doorway holding the biggest knife I have in the house. My eyes almost lunge out their sockets when I recognize the knife. I try to free myself from bondage again because my life truly depends on it. She could dice me into one hundred pieces and there would be nothing I could do about it.

"I don't know what you're planning to do with that, but I hope you don't plan on cutting me with it," I nervously state.

Cassie doesn't reply orally, but does give me a sinister look. She approaches the bed and starts to drag the knife along the bed. I'm terrified out of my mind as I attempt to kick my legs and scream. She climbs on top of me and pokes me lightly several times with the knife, but doesn't draw any blood. This is some crazy shit! Cassie holds the knife to my neck and the raises it above my face as she grips the handle of the knife with both hands.

She's gripping the knife as if she intends to ram it into my face or chest. I'm helpless like a rat stuck in a trap. I can't defend myself beyond screaming and it's a sickening feeling. This feeling of helplessness is truly a first for me. I've always prided myself in be strong and never vulnerable, but that is not the case in this moment. I'm more exposed than I've ever been in my life and now is when I have the most to lose. My current predicament may cost me my life. I realize there's nothing I can do, so I just close my eyes and cry. I don't want to see what's about to happen. I just hope she doesn't torture me.

"Please, just make it quick!" I utter as I whimper.

"Make it quick, you say. Well, that totally depends on you. If you give me what I want, this will be short and painless. I'll cut you free of the scarves and you won't be harmed. However, if you don't give me what I want immediately, it'll be a very long and gruesome night for you. I promise you that things are going to get very messy," Cassie states as she eyeballs me.

"Give you what you want? Well, what the hell do you want from me?" I inquire urgently.

"Yes, give me what I want! You have a symbolic chain around my neck and it's choking the life out of me slowly. Don't play dumb with me Kim. You know what the fuck I want. I need the evidence that you have implicating me in Russell's murder and I need it now," Cassie tells as she pokes the knife into my pillow.

I reply calmly, "Cassie, please untie me, so we

can talk about this civilly. Having me tied to this bed like a prisoner doesn't make me feel comfortable about what you might do to me even if I tell you where the evidence is."

"Bitch, you essentially have me framed for Russell's murder and you're talking about not feeling comfortable! That's laughable. I should cut off one of your damn lips, so you can't continue to spew so much bullshit!" Cassie words angrily.

Cassie rubs the tip of the knife on my bottom lip and pokes it. Next, she asks me which lip I want to part ways with. I don't answer because I'm terrified and I really don't want to choose which lip to lose. Normally, I'm not afraid of anything, but in this situation, I am because I know Cassie will cut me up. I feel she'll deliver on her threat because she's like me in thought and I know I'd surely cut someone up if they had such damning evidence against me.

I have to handle this conundrum just right otherwise I'm minced meat. What would make me not continue on with something like this? I'd most likely feed on the weakness someone displayed in this situation, so I can't show weakness. I have to be strong and confident to make it out of here alive. I have to be more strategic than I've ever been.

"Fuck it! You know what Cassie? Fuck it! Cut both of my damn lips off and when you finish that, be sure to drive that knife straight through my heart! If I can't live with you by my side, I don't want to live at all. In fact, untie my hand and I'll kill my damn self," I voice sternly.

She speaks, "Okay, fine. It's your choice. I'm gonna cut your lips off and feed them to you. Let's see how you like that. I think you're going to hate it terribly and then I'll figure out what else I can do to you. You'll be begging me to stop and you'll give me that evidence for sure or you'll be begging me to just kill you."

Cassie slaps me across the face and giggles. Next, she grabs one of the pillows on the bed and puts it over my face. She lightly presses the pillow down on my face. I know where this is going, so I wiggle my head back and forth to try to shake the pillow off. Unfortunately, my efforts are to no avail because the pillow isn't budging. I realize that I'm exerting a tremendous amount of energy for nothing, so I stop. Cassie puts more pressure on the pillow and now breathing is becoming difficult. I can't believe this is how it's going to end for me. I wonder what the headlines will say.

Cassie says, while pressing harder as the seconds tick, "You know you can't hold your breath forever, so you might as well give me what I seek. I kid you not; you'll be losing consciousness very soon. It doesn't have to be this way. Just come clean."

I feel myself slipping in and out, but I feel a gush of fresh air hit my nostrils. The feeling is exhilarating. I never knew how precious breathing air was until this moment. Gladly, Cassie removed the pillow from my face. I'm hoping she had a change of heart.

"Do you still want to keep where the evidence is a secret?" Cassie asks.

I reply, "Yes, but let me…"

To my dismay, Cassie puts the pillow back over my face and continues to suffocate me again. I hold my breath and hope that she pulls the pillow up again. I've always been able to hold my breath for long periods of time. Maybe if I start out squirming and then stop she'll think I'm dead. If she thinks she killed me, she may leave the house. I'll still be tied up, but at least I'll be alive. Someone may come looking for me and save me. I put my plan into action. I shake for a moment and then I stop. When I stop moving, Cassie stops pressing the pillow over my face, but she doesn't remove it. I'm glad she doesn't remove the pillow from covering my face because it allows me to breath without being detected.

Cassie gets off the bed and I can hear her moving around my room. She's opening and closing drawers. Next, I hear her rummaging through my closet. It becomes apparent that she's looking for something. My guess is that she's looking for the evidence that I have against her. The funny thing is that she doesn't know exactly what to look for. I continue to play dead while I figure out what my escape plan is. Cassie plops back on the bed. Part of me wants to say something to her, but I decide not to. Playing dead is keeping me alive, so I'll continue doing it.

"Kim, I know you're not dead, so you can cut the charade," Cassie says as she takes the pillow from over my face.

"How'd you know?" I ask.

She doesn't answer my question. What she does next scares the hell out of me.

Cassie starts screaming at the top of her lungs. The scream she is letting out is deafening. I open my eyes back up and see that Cassie has a steady stream of tears running down her face. She seems to be more conflicted, disgruntled, and messed up than I am. Cassie jumps off the bed and cuts one of the scarves from the bedpost, but doesn't untie the others. Instead, she exits the room and disappears out of my line of sight. I don't know where she went, but I'm not going to wait for her to come back with another weapon. I can reach my arm that's still tied up, so I untie the scarf. Next, I release my legs from bondage as well. My arms and legs are pretty burned from where the scarves were tied.

The silk cut through my skin pretty good, but at least I'm free now. I know at any moment Cassie could be back with another weapon, so I decide to arm myself. I reach in my nightstand and grab a gun that belonged to Russell. I stealthily move through the house to see if I see Cassie. I'll surely kill her if she tries me. I search all of my rooms upstairs, but am unable to locate her, so I go downstairs. When I make it down the stairs, I hear water running. I can tell the sound of the running water is coming from the bathroom.

I kick the bathroom door open and peer inside. I see Cassie sitting in the tub with the shower water running on her while she's fully clothed. She's now holding the knife to her throat and sobbing viciously. I point the gun at her for my own safety.

"What the hell is wrong with you?" I inquire.

She replies, "Nothing is wrong. I'm fine."

"Clearly, you're not fine. Cassie, you had me scared as hell when you had the knife to my throat, but now I'm even more terrified that you have it to yours. You need to put the knife down," I communicate.

She speaks crazily, "I'll put it down alright. Down my fucking throat!"

I verbalize, "You don't want to do that, so just put it down please."

"How the hell you know that I don't want to do it?" Cassie asks.

I calmly answer, "I know that because you just had the same knife to my neck and you didn't stab me, so I know you don't want to stab yourself either. In fact, if you put the knife down, I'll put the gun down, then we'll talk. Cassie, you mean too much to me for me to let you hurt yourself."

Something I said to her was moving because she throws the knife out of the tub on to the floor. I pick the knife up and put my gun in its holster. I walk over to the tub and turn off the shower water. Next, I wrap my hands around Cassie and stand her up and she steps out of the tub. I strip her of her soaked clothes, grab a towel off the rack, and dry her wet body off. We exit the bathroom and walk to the kitchen to talk. I fix two cups of coffee.

"Now, I know you said you were fine, but we both know that's not true, so it's time for you to spill the beans," I articulate.

"Right, I guess it's blatantly obvious that I'm fucked up right now," Cassie agrees.

"Obvious is an understatement. What's wrong with you?" I quiz.

"Everything is wrong! This is wrong! That's wrong! I'm really fucked up out here. I don't know what the hell is going on," Cassie rambles.

"Girl, I don't know what the hell is going on either. I really have no idea what you're talking about. You need to be more clear!" I remark confusedly.

"I know I'm talking and acting crazy. Hell, I'm thinking crazy too, but what I was trying to say is that all of this has me very confused to the point that I feel lost. Listen, I'm conflicted because I love being with you and the things we do are very dear to my heart," Cassie conveys affectionately.

"I'm glad you feel that way because I do too,"

I insist.

Cassie utters, "Please let me finish before I lose my train of thought. Now, with that being said, I'm also very conflicted because of what happened to Russell and I'm also bothered by the fact that you basically forced me into this relationship with you. My heart is happy, but my mind is all fucked up. If this would've happened over regular circumstances, I wouldn't have so much internal conflict, but this didn't happen naturally."

"I understand how you could be so mentally twisted because I often think about the way it went down and wish it could have been a different way, but it wasn't. What helps me sleep at night is that I find comfort in the result of everything that transpired. I'm with you and that makes me happier than anything. My best advice for you is to let the past go and live in the present and for the future. Our future is looking pretty damn bright," I narrate.

"It's not that easy for me all the time. Sometimes I can block the past out, but other times I can't. I think all the time that Russell is dead because of me," Cassie words.

I respond, "If you feel guilty about Russell's death, you shouldn't. I say that because it's really his fault that all of this happened. He should have never agreed to the threesome the night of his party. He opened the door for his tragic demise. Besides, he always said that he didn't want to live without me and he doesn't. I wanted to just leave him to be with you, but since he always said he didn't want to live without me, I killed him. I simply gave him what he wanted. We'll just call it an assisted suicide."

"Since you put it like that, it was slightly his fault. Well, I feel a little better about things since you broke it down for me," Cassie mentions as she sips some coffee.

We talk further about the situation. I'm glad I'm able to disarm her ill feelings and inner turmoil about all that has happened. I almost lost my mind and heart when she turned the knife on herself. The crazy thing is that I was more horrified by Cassie having the knife to her own throat than when she had it to mine. The thing is that I really love Cassie. Russell always told me that he couldn't live without me and I feel exactly the same way about Cassie. She is my sole reason for breathing at this point.

I would hope that she knows I did all of this for her. Russell was in the way of Cassie and me being together, so he had to be eliminated. I know I forced her into this relationship, but I had to win her over and it worked. I've always been a woman who's driven by attaining the results I want. Now, Cassie loves me and all I have to do is continue to nurture our relationship. I explain to her that I had to use coercion to be with her on the front end because she wasn't giving me valid consideration. After hours of talking about all that has happened between us, we go back upstairs to my bedroom. Cassie tells me that she's tired and not in the mood for any sexual activities, so she just wants to cuddle. I'm fine with that because cuddling is intimate in its own right and I want Cassie to know that our relationship is bigger than sex. This night didn't go the way I expected it to go, but at least we're together. We fall asleep while holding one another in our arms.

CHAPTER 12

It's so crazy how busy I've been lately. I was thinking I was busy when Russell was alive, but I was mistaken. I wish I had as much free time now as I did just a short while ago. I never imagined that Russell's career would posthumously blossom as much as it has. I estimated that his book sales would rise twenty or twenty-five percent, but this is ridiculous. His sales have risen seventy-five percent in the time since he was killed. I'm really raking it in now!

Even though I suspected his sales would go up, I never imagined in my wildest dreams what it would do for my career. I've been doing interviews all over the place and being compensated for them. Of course, I've done an interview for Cassie's magazine too. I can honestly say that I'm a great actress. It seems like America really loves the story of loss and depression over my husband's death. If they knew I was the one who did it, they'd turn their backs on me for sure. I'm glad that's not the case. Another thing I didn't expect to come from this, is that I've been approached by three different authors who are interested in turning my story into a novel. How funny is that?

Additionally, a new internet movie streaming company wants to turn Russell's novel series into a series for their network. The money they are offering is on another level. This deal will ensure that I'll be able to spend money how I want and never have to worry about going broke. I will have a lot of say so in the production of the series. Going forward, I plan to turn that into another career for myself. Russell always told me to seize every opportunity that comes my way and I'm doing just that.

I was hoping to link up with Cassie today, but sadly, I will not. She's entertaining some new clients today, so she's going to be tied up. I have the worst luck sometimes. I say that because I'm free today and won't be free again anytime soon that I know of. Oh well, it is what it is. I have to pay a storage bill at Union Station, so I'm here now. I'm not going to be in here for long. It's just a quick in and out for me. I walk over to the locker storage counter to pay my fee. Fortunately, there is no line, so I'm all paid up and leaving in no time.

I walk away from the locker storage counter

and hear someone calling my name. I've heard that voice a thousand times and immediately recognize it as being Cassie's voice. What in the world is she doing here? She told me that she'd be busy with clients all day. I turn around and confirm what my ears had already told me. It's Cassie and she's heading right towards me. I walk in her direction and we meet.

"Girl, you are the last person I expected to see here!" I say.

Cassie responds enthusiastically, "Chile, I know that's right! I didn't want to be here. This is not the place for me."

"Well, what brings you here?" I ask.

"Girl, the only thing that would get me here is what has me here…work. The client I'm meeting today didn't want to fly into town, so he decided to catch the damn train. Got me down here in all this traffic and with all these people just for his train to be late," Cassie explains.

"Oh, okay. I know train stations aren't your style, so it surprised the hell outta me when I heard you calling me. Well, I'm glad I got to see you. Call me later if you're free," I reply as I try to rush away.

"I will… but you don't have to run away so quickly. I'm trying to figure out what you're doing here. Hell, Union Station isn't exactly a chill spot for you," Cassie mentions.

I speak, "Oh, I wasn't trying to run off quickly. I just wasn't trying to be pushy and stick around knowing you have business to tend to. I didn't want to impose."

"I understand that. What brings you down here to where the commoners are?" Cassie asks jokingly.

"Umm, nothing really. I just wanted to get out of the house for a while. Didn't really feel like being by myself, so I came down here," I reply dishonestly.

"Shit, I know sometimes I don't want to be alone, but I ain't never brought my ass down here. I normally go to a bookstore or to the movies, but never down here. However, to each his own," Cassie comments.

"Right, we're all different," I shoot back.

Cassie's phone starts ringing and she pulls it out of her handbag and answers it. I wait patiently while she takes the call. Fortunately, the call is very brief because I want to get out of here as soon as possible. Cassie tells me that her client is off the train and is looking for her, so she needs to go. I don't hold her up another minute. She walks toward the escalators leading from the train tracks. Reluctantly, I exit the building. Even though I want to go back to the storage locker, I don't because it's in the direction of the tracks and I don't want Cassie to see me again. My best bet is to go home and have a drink to calm my nerves.

I wish I was able to tell if Cassie thought my story about being in Union Station was bullshit or not because if I knew, my nerves wouldn't be shot to hell. Damn, I know she's very perceptive and isn't easily fooled. I wonder if she paid any attention to the fact that I was coming from the stored luggage area. I wish I would've seen her first, so I'd know for sure what she saw. Since Cassie saw me first, it's possible that she saw me at the counter paying for more storage time. I'm really considering moving that bag to another location. I really don't have another location to store the evidence incriminating Cassie of Russell's murder.

I definitely can't have it here with me at home because that would be entirely too risky. What if Cassie really didn't question why I was by the luggage check area? What if I'm overreacting like I've been known to do? Even if Cassie did notice what I was doing, she couldn't access the box without me. I'm clear either way. Hell, what if she calls the authorities and has them check the box. If they get their hands on that bag, I'm finished for sure. On the other hand, Cassie's DNA was found at Russell's murder scene, so even if she did call the cops and make them aware of the bag, it would only incriminate her. With all of the evidence stacked against her, there's no way they wouldn't prosecute her. The only question is if they would prosecute me as an accomplice to the murder. Well, I'm not chancing that.

Damn, there's so many ways this scenario

could play out. I think it's in my best interest to get the bag out of the storage locker. I don't want to take a chance on going to jail, so I have to move the bag. I won't sleep comfortably if I don't. If I discard the bag altogether, that will ensure I don't have to worry about any issues with the law, but on the other hand, I won't have any leverage on Cassie to stay in a relationship with me. I refuse to lose her. I'll just move the bag to another storage locker in D.C. That's the best move for me.

I have some calls to make and other business to handle pertaining to my publishing company, so I tend to that. I'll wait until it's dark out before I go back to Union Station to retrieve the bag. I noticed that they have a crew for the day shift at the locker storage area and a totally different crew for the night shift. Going at different times of the day when different staff members are there reduces the chances of one employee recognizing me. If I go at the same time, there's a better chance of my face becoming known to them.

Hours have gone by and I'm ready to get to the station. I really couldn't sit still because my mind was a wreck. I even texted Cassie a couple of times to see where she was, but she never responded. That really drove me crazy. For all I know, she's at the locker right now. Why didn't she just answer me back to put my mind at ease? Hell, I've cleaned this house three times today out of sheer nervousness. Fuck waiting any longer! I'm going now before I have a heart attack.

I switch my outfit to a less flamboyant one. I throw my hair in a ponytail and put on a baseball cap. I grab a small luggage bag and my purse and head out the door. I park my car and head inside of Union Station. I walk inside the station with my head down like nothing is awry. I know there are a million cameras in here, so I'm not helping myself any by hiding my face. In fact, acting unnaturally will make me seem suspicious. I definitely don't want that. As I walk to the storage area, I hear a police officer walking behind me while talking on the phone.

What the hell is he doing in here? Is he here for me? I'm not turning around if he doesn't say anything to me. I'm surely not walking to the storage area with a police officer potentially trailing me. That's not going to happen. I continue walking straight and then turn in the opposite direction of the storage area. I walk to the corner of the sitting area where I have a clear line of sight of the storage area. As suspected, the cop goes to the storage area. Damn, he's on to me for sure. I know I shouldn't be staring so hard over there, but I can't help myself. My eyes are fixed on what's going on like an eagle's eyes on its prey. I wish I could hear what he's saying. I can tell he's asking for something, but what exactly I don't know. Oh shit, he's investigating something because now the manager is over there talking to him.

Fuck! It's time for me to get my ass out of here. I want to keep looking, but I know this place could be flooded with police officers at any minute. As I stand up to leave, I look back over at the storage counter and I'm surprised by what I see. To my surprise, the officer is handed a bag by the attendant. The best part about it is that it isn't the bag that I put in storage. He apparently put a bag of his own in storage. I can't help but to laugh out loud at myself. I'm so paranoid about all of this and it's causing me to think the world has formed a cabal against me.

The officer waves goodbye to the clerk and walks off. I start walking over to the counter to get the bag with the items I used to orchestrate Russell's murder. As I'm walking to the counter, I see the beautiful face of Cassie Monroe. She's strutting quickly and confidently through the terminal. Cassie is walking with intent. I can clearly tell that she's on a mission. I can't figure out why she's in here again. I don't see her with a client and it's not likely that she's meeting one this late, so it's odd that she's in here. I decide to sit tight and not approach Cassie as she's walking because I want to see where she's going.

Cassie walks over to the counter where my luggage is being stored and begins talking to the attendant. There's no way she has a bag stored there. I need to see what business she has over there. My intuition tells me that she's up to no good. I walk over to the counter area and stand out of Cassie's view, but can hear all that's going on.

"I'm here to pick up my bag," Cassie says to the clerk.

"Okay, Ma'am, I'll be glad to get your bag for you. I'll need your ticket please," the clerk responds.

"Oh, the ticket. I seem to have misplaced it, but I'll give you my name and you can get it that way. My name is Kim Davenport," Cassie tells the attendant.

My stomach receives a deep sharp pain that I can't shake. I now know that Cassie is on to me. She's always been very perceptive, so when she saw me here, she didn't buy my made-up story. I knew she wouldn't. I'm just glad she didn't come back with the cops to get the bag out of storage. She probably didn't tell them anything about it because she wants to discard of the items herself. It makes sense because she would be incriminating herself by bringing forth the evidence in the bag. Also, she doesn't know if there's really anything in the locker, so she could possibly bring the cops down here for nothing.

I anxiously wait to hear what the attendant is going to tell her. This is going to be interesting to say the least. Will she break protocol or will she follow company policy? My guess is that she's going to break policy, but I'm not worried about it one bit. I'm always impressed by how smooth

Cassie is. I guess that's why I fell in love with her. When I see Cassie, it's like I'm looking in the mirror and seeing myself.

The attendant replies, "If you don't have your ticket, I can't release your bag to you. I'm sorry, but it's company policy. Look at the sign ma'am. I could lose my job."

Cassie speaks, "I know what your sign says, but I really need my bag. It means the world to me. I just need you to help me out this one time. I'll even throw you a few dollars for your troubles."

"I'll do you a favor this one time and I'll need one hundred dollars for breaking the rules. Give me your identification, describe the bag, and tell me the contents of the bag. If you do those things, I'll release the bag to you," the clerk words.

Cassie pulls out the one hundred dollars, but does not produce her identification and doesn't describe the bag. She knows that she's hit a brick wall. There's no way she can produce identification with my name on it or describe a bag that she's never seen. I wasn't worried about her getting the bag because I have the ticket needed to access the locker with me. She tries to manipulate the attendant with more money.

Cassie speaks sternly, "Listen, I don't have time for all of that. Here's the money and an extra one hundred dollars. Now, go get the bag that corresponds with my name."

The lady takes the money and puts it in her pocket. Next, she tells Cassie that she still needs to describe the bag for her because she doesn't have the ticket. It would take too long trying to find out which bag it is because there are so many bags. Cassie doesn't like her answer, but realizes the truth of what she is being told. Cassie is defeated because she can't point the clerk in the right direction to find the bag.

Cassie asks, "When do you work again?"

"I work tomorrow night at the same time," she answers.

"That's good! I'll be back tomorrow night. By then, you should have had enough time to find the bag that correlates to Kim Davenport. If you find it, I'll give you another thousand dollars for helping me out," Cassie voices.

The clerk's eyes almost pop out of her eye sockets when Cassie promises her a thousand dollars for finding the bag. The clerk assures Cassie that she'll have the bag by then. Cassie thanks her for her help and walks off. I stay hidden until Cassie leaves the terminal. My mind is spinning rapidly. What a bitch Cassie is! She's trying to double deal. She's just like me and I love her more for it. She's equipped with a devilish mind just like me. She wants the bag at all costs and I don't blame her for it. I'm slightly turned on by her scheming mind. Cassie tried to steal my evidence right from under me. I giggle to myself at how cunning Cassie is as I approach the counter. I swear, I see more of her ways in me as the days go on.

CHAPTER 13

Last night at Union Station got very interesting to say the least. I went from quietly picking my bag up from storage to thinking the cops were following me only to find out the Cassie was on to the bag being stashed. I'm glad I actually went up there when I did and was able to get ahead of things. Hell, I almost got caught with my pants down. Oh well, I didn't get caught up and today is a new day filled with new happenings.

I've been running around all day attending to my publishing company's affairs. I haven't had a moment to myself since I awoke. The life of an entrepreneur is never a simple one. At least I'm on the better side of all of it. I only have one last stop to make and then I can go home. I'm driving back to Union Station to see what happens when Cassie arrives. I know I should just go home and relax, but my curious nature won't let me to that. I have to see this thing play out to its end.

I pull into the parking lot and park my car. I get out and walk inside. I sit in the same seat I was in last night that gave me a perfect view of what was going on at the storage counter. There's nothing going on over there and is business as usual. About ten minutes later, two officers storm Union Station and approach the storage counter. I can see that one of the officers is Detective Patrick Jones. He's the lead investigator on Russell's murder case. I'm elated to see him over there. I don't recognize the other officer who's accompanying him.

I can tell that they're asking the staff at the counter a lot of questions. The lady who is currently at the counter is the same one who was there last night when Cassie and I were here. I don't see any other officers trailing them, so I go to the same hiding spot I was in last night that allows me to hear what's going on without being seen. I overhear the cops asking the clerk if she knows the lady in the photo that they are showing her. She tells them that she doesn't recognize the woman in the photo.

"Ma'am, we received a tip that there is some evidence in one of these lockers that's crucial to our investigation. Look at this picture closely please. Don't be so dismissive," Detective Jones says.

She states, "I'm not being dismissive. I don't

recognize that lady, but a lady came in last night to pick up her bag, but didn't have the ticket for me to release it to her. She said her name was Kim Davenbridge or something like that. She was very pressed about it."

"Is that right? Well, is there any way we can see the security footage of the counter from last night? Is there any possibility that the lady's name was Kim Davenport?" Patrick Jones asks.

She replies, "Yes, yes, that's her name! Kim Davenport. I knew it was something like that. As far as the security tape for the counter, our system has a virus and isn't functioning."

"Damn it! I thought we were one step closer to having her," the other officer says to Detective Jones.

"We are. According to the clerk, she didn't release the bag to her. That would mean that the bag is still in the back somewhere," Detective Jones speaks.

"Yes, the bag is in there somewhere, but I have no way of finding it without the ticket. I mean there are a whole lot of bags back there. The tag will send me directly to its location," explains the clerk.

"I understand. Well, there has to be some way to locate the bag easily. If we look at the list of names, that should get us on the right track," Patrick Jones remarks.

"Not necessarily because the names don't often correlate to a bag's location and the correct name may not be on the tag that's on the bag. Listen, you guys can just wait for her to show up tonight. She's supposed to come back tonight to pick the bag up," the attendant tells.

"Now, how do you know that?" inquires Detective Jones.

"Easy, she told me last night that she'd be back for the bag in about thirty minutes from now," the clerk informs.

The two officers are happy to hear that who they think is me will be back to pick the checked bag up. They know that Union Station is near where Russell was killed, so they begin to think that I could've stashed the murder weapon here and drove home. It makes sense that they think I did it because I had the most to gain from Russell's death. The two cops decide they need to move away from the counter because they don't want me to see them when I walk up. Even though the clerk didn't tell them she recognized me from the photo they showed her, they still don't believe her. They think she's mistaken.

They decide to wait in the back of the storage area for me to show up. They want to catch me red-handed with the bag. They know if they catch me with some damning evidence, there's no way I can refute it. I decide to go back to my seat and wait for Cassie to arrive. Like clockwork, thirty minutes later, Cassie arrives. The hair on the back of my neck stands up when I see her walking towards the counter. As she nears the counter, I get up and walk back over to my hidden location that allows me to hear what's going on.

"Hi, my name is Kim Davenport. I'm here to pick my bag up," Cassie says assertively.

"Yes, I remember you from last night. I'll go in the back and get that for you," the clerk tells.

A few minutes later, she returns from getting the bag and hands it over to Cassie. Cassie zips the bag open just enough to look inside and sees some bloody clothing and a sterling silver letter opener. The letter opener is monogrammed to her, so she knows it's hers. She smiles a grin of satisfaction and relief because she knows I no longer have any leverage over her. Cassie Monroe feels that she has her life back. Unfortunately, she has no idea what misfortune looms ahead. Cassie places an envelope with one thousand dollars on the counter and the clerk quickly picks it up and hides it.

"Have a good night, Mrs. Davenport," the attendant says. "I'm glad I was able to help you with your bag.

Cassie replies as she winks at me, "Thank you. I couldn't have found my bag without you. You have a good night too!"

"Oh yeah, one more thing before you go," the clerk states.

"Yeah? What's that?" Cassie asks.

The two officers walk out from their hiding places and stop Cassie. Now, this is the moment

I've been waiting for. This is why I couldn't go home. I wouldn't have missed this for the world. I see Detective Jones's face and he's surprised to see someone other than me standing there. Both officers have very confused looks on their faces. I'm grinning from ear to ear. However, Cassie isn't smiling. She has a look of confusion and terror on her face as she notices the officers' badges.

"Hi, ma'am. My name is Detective Jones and this is Officer Wright. We're with the D.C. Police Department. We're investigating a murder and believe evidence pertinent to our investigation may be in that bag," Detective Jones explains.

"Okay, nice to meet you, but I don't have anything to do with any murder. I'm so sorry to hear that," Cassie utters.

"What's your name ma'am? And what's in the bag?" Patrick Jones asks.

"My name is Kim Davenport. As far as this bag goes, it's none of your business," Cassie snaps back angrily.

"That's interesting because I know a woman with the exact same name, but you're not her. Let me see some identification," Detective Jones says. "You're mistaken. That bag is plenty of our business."

"Well unless you're telling me that I've done something or you have a warrant to search me or an arrest warrant, I'll be on my merry damn way. My lawyer would love to hear about you detaining me for no apparent reason," Cassie words.

"I'm glad you're Kim Davenport because I have a search warrant for your property. Here it is freshly signed by Judge Carter," speaks Patrick Jones.

Officer Wright grabs the bag and pries it from Cassie grip. She's doesn't want to let it go, but her grip eventually gives out. Once she realizes she's in tremendous trouble, she attempts to tell the truth. She screams that she's not really Kim Davenport and that her name is really Cassie Monroe. Many people are standing around to see what's transpiring. Detective Jones opens the bag and sees its contents. They proceed to arrest Cassie. They read her rights and take her into custody. I hide in the crowd until they drag her away. She cries as they continue reading her rights to her. I go home and go to sleep.

It's the morning and I slept great. I still can't believe how well that went last night. Cassie impersonated me and got caught red-handed with all the evidence that the prosecutor will need to convict her of Russell's murder. I'm sure at some point they'll get her DNA sample and match it to the DNA found on the gloves I left at the scene of the murder. The case will be open and shut for sure.

Apparently, Cassie has one hell of a lawyer because she bonded out of jail and I have several missed calls from her. I listen to the messages she left and they're all beyond threatening. She's even sent four extremely violent text messages to me. She's claiming that she's going to get her revenge on me and that this situation isn't over. I'm not following her up at this point. She's going down faster than a two-dollar whore. I don't respond to any of the messages because it's not in my best interest.

I'm sure she won't take being ignored lightly. In fact, it wouldn't surprise me if she showed up at my house. For the most part, Cassie and I think very similarly and I know what I'd do if the situation were reversed. I go down to the kitchen and prepare some coffee. I need a caffeine rush to wake myself up. While the coffee is brewing, I walk outside to get the newspaper. I go back inside to hear my phone ringing back to back with calls from Cassie. I don't know if I should be afraid or not. Moments later, my coffee finishes brewing. The aroma of the coffee has infiltrated my kitchen. One French vanilla coffee coming right up! I sip the coffee and it tastes unusually delicious. Maybe it's the taste of victory.

As I savor every sip of my coffee and flip through the pages of the paper, my doorbell starts ringing accompanied by thunderous knocking at the door. I pick up my tablet to access my security camera and see that it's Cassie on my porch. Oh my goodness. How could someone be so damn predictable? I can't believe I fell for someone who's so damn weak. I'm almost embarrassed to think that I thought we were alike. I bet she wants answers to why I did her the way I did, but she's not going to get any answers from me. For all I know, she's wearing a wire and is trying to set me up.

Cassie screams, while continuing to bang on the door, "Open the door bitch!"

I yell back, "Get away from my door bitch! You're not welcome here, so I'd appreciate it tremendously if you'd leave now."

I decide that yelling at Cassie through the door is pointless. Unfortunately, her verbal assaults only get worse. I figure it's in my best interest to call the police now. I place the call to 911 and inform them that an intruder is on my doorstep threatening me. The 911 operator hears the banging on the door and tells me to retreat somewhere in my house until the cops arrive. As I walk into my room to hide, I hear the sound of my door opening.

How can she really be this predictable? I didn't lock the door after I retrieved my newspaper on purpose. I yell for Cassie to get out of my house. I'm still on the phone with the 911 operator and inform her that Cassie has entered my home. The operator reiterates her directive for me to hide and tells me not to hang up the phone.

"Ma'am, the police are on their way. We have a unit two minutes away. Lock yourself in the bathroom or something and hold tight," the 911 dispatch says.

"Okay, I will, but tell the cops to hurry because she's after me and I'm terrified," I voice to the operator.

Cassie runs up the steps after me and is still screaming irately. I'm not panicked one bit because I know she's all bark and no bite. I make it to my bedroom and slam the door closed behind me, but I don't lock it. I throw the phone on my bed and grab Russell's gun. Cassie bursts through the door and sees me pointing the gun directly at her. She looks at me in an astonished fashion. I can tell by the look on her face that she knows that she's been set up. I smile a devilish grin at her because I know I've won again and this time it's for good.

I scream as I pull the trigger several times, "Don't hurt me! Please, don't hurt me!"

Each bullet I shoot at Cassie, hits her in her upper torso. She falls to the floor and lands with a loud thud. There are blood and guts all over the place. The 911 operator hears the shots and calls out for me. I drop the gun where I'm standing and rush to the phone.

"Hello, hello," I say frantically as I pick the phone back up.

The dispatch asks, "Mrs. Davenport, are you still there? I heard gunshots, what happened?"

"Yes, I'm…I'm here. I had to shoot her. I think she's dead because she's not moving and there's blood everywhere," I answer in a shaken tone. "I need the cops here now."

"Stay calm Mrs. Davenport. The cops are on your block now. They'll be there any second. I need you to put the gun down, so the cops don't think you're a threat," she states.

I voice while pretending to weep, "The gun is on the floor. I dropped it. I'm gonna go downstairs and wait for them. I can't stay in this room looking at her dead like this."

"I understand ma'am," she responds.

I walk downstairs and wait on my porch. The police pull up and jump out the car. One cop asks me if I'm alright and asks where the intruder is. I tell them she's in the bedroom at the top of the stairs to the left. They tell me to stay outside while they storm the house. Moments later, one cop emerges and informs me that Cassie is dead. I act like I didn't know for sure, but I emptied the magazine into her, so I knew her life had come to an end.

The officer consoles me and asks me if I'm prepared to give a statement as to what happened. I tell him step by step what happened as he writes the information down. More cops pull up and go inside my home. It really looks like a movie murder scene around here. I just have to remain cool until this interrogation is over. I know I'm going to need new carpet for sure. What color should I get? Hell, maybe I'll move altogether.

The officer says, "Ma'am! Ma'am! I asked you

a question."

"I'm sorry. My mind was drifting. You know, with all that has happened here tonight," I speak.

"Oh, I know this is a lot, but I asked if you knew the intruder," the cop verbalizes.

"Yes, I knew her," I answer.

The cop asks me to detail how I knew Cassie, so I do just that. I don't leave out any details. I tell them about the nights that me, Russell, and Cassie shared as well as the fling that Cassie and I had after Russell's murder. The cop is all ears and is writing everything down. While we're talking, Detective Jones pulls up and walks to the porch. I knew he'd be arriving at some point. I'm sure he heard either my name or Cassie's name over his radio and rushed right over.

Detective Jones talks to the cop who was interviewing me for a few minutes to get briefed on the situation. Next, he goes inside to see Cassie's body and the crime scene. Patrick Jones comes back downstairs and calls me into the kitchen. We talk about all that has happened tonight with Cassie as well as the past. I tell him the exact same story that I told the other officer. I can't deviate from the story because I'm sure Detective Jones thinks that Russell's murder and now Cassie's killing is somehow my fault. I don't even let on that I know that Cassie was arrested for Russell's murder.

"Kim, I don't know if you know this or not, but Cassie Monroe was arrested last night for the murder of your husband. I didn't get a chance to call you because it happened so late," he tells.

"What?! You can't be serious!" I utter in a shocked tone.

"I'm very serious. I wish I wasn't serious, but I am. Last night we received a tip about her involvement in Russell's murder and it turned out to be a pretty good tip. I can't tell you anymore about it because the investigation is ongoing," he responds.

"I understand, but that's crazy as hell that she turns up here," I say.

"Yes, it is crazy to say the least. With that being said, do you know why she would wish to cause Russell or you harm?" the detective inquires.

"I really don't know. Like I told the officer, Russell, Cassie, and I had a couple of threesomes and she consoled me after Russell died, but I don't know why she'd want to harm us," I explain.

"Okay, if you have anything else you want to share with us, don't hesitate to call me. You already have my card," Detective Jones says.

"Yes, I still have it. This entire ordeal has my nerves bad. Oh, I do have the security footage of what happened tonight. I forgot to mention it to the other officer, I explain.

Detective Jones wants to see exactly what happened and is elated that I have the footage of what went down. I tell him that it's all captured on my tablet, but it's in my room. He goes to my room to retrieve it. I unlock it and rewind the film to when Cassie was initially banging on my front door. He calls another officer over to look at it with him. They both look with intense scrutiny at the video. The video captures everything up until Cassie enters my bedroom because Russell and I didn't want security cameras in our bedroom.

Detective Jones finishes watching the video and tells me that he's going to need this footage for evidence. According to him, the video surveillance makes this case open and shut. I know once they couple the 911 call with the surveillance video they will deem what I did to be self-defense for sure. I'm not surprised one bit. Also, all the evidence against Cassie will remove any suspicion from my name. After a few hours, the cops, coroner, and other personnel all leave.

EPILOGUE

It's been weeks since I killed Cassie. I haven't been back in my bedroom since it all went down. As we speak, I have some men cleaning up the place and doing some renovations. I've spent the last two weeks at the Empire Hotel. I find it hilarious that this is the place where it all started. It seems like that night was eons ago. I feel like I'm a completely different person from that night. Maybe I'm not really different, but my life is and will be different from now on.

Detective Jones called me earlier today and told me that he closed the investigation into Russell's death. According to him, they had a large cache of evidence pointing in the direction of Cassie as being the murderer of Russell. He told me that the evidence they found on Cassie had Russell's DNA on it and the gloves that were left at the murder scene had both of their DNA on it. When I asked him about Cassie's murder, he told me that it was ruled to be self-defense and that I was free and clear of all charges. The conversation only confirmed everything that I knew it would. The conversation was short and sweet.

I essentially killed two people and got away with it. Hell, I essentially got paid to kill them because I got all of the money from our company and the life insurance money from Russell's death. Next, I'll be suing Cassie's magazine company in a wrongful death lawsuit for Russell's homicide. I'm sure her company will settle with me instead of fighting a battle they can't win. A good plan will never fail and a few dollars well spent can go very far.

I have to meet with the clerk that was at the luggage storage counter at Union Station. I was able to work out a deal with her to help me with the Cassie situation. I offered her ten thousand dollars to not mention that the bag really belonged to me. Additionally, I gave her a script to follow for when the police arrived. I must say that she played the part to perfection. You may ask who sent the tip to the police about the evidence from Russell's murder being in storage. Well, that was yours truly! I did that. I had to get Cassie and the police down there at the same time, so they'd catch Cassie red-handed.

It's 10 p.m. and the clerk is waiting for me in the parking garage for me to give her the money I owe her. I'm dressed in black leggings, black sneakers, and an all-black hoodie. I walk over to the girl's car and she looks up at me. She rolls down the window, so we can do our business. I hand her an envelope filled with money. She smiles widely.

"Go ahead and count it," I order. "I want you to know that I'm a woman of my word and it's all there."

"Okay, I'll count it. I'll be honest, I was kinda skeptical about you showing up to pay me," the girl says.

"No, I wouldn't do you like that. You really helped me out and I appreciate you for that," I convey.

The girl opens the envelope and starts to count the cash. While her attention is on the money, I take half of a brick out of my pocket and knock her upside the head with it. The money falls to her lap as she slumps over unconscious. I pick the money up and put it in my pocket. I bash her upside the head several more times until she's dead. I turn around and walk casually out of the parking garage. I walk several blocks away from the garage to my car and drive home. I take off all my articles of clothing and throw them into my burning hot fireplace. After that, I get in the shower.

I finish showering and fix myself a drink. I really didn't want to kill the girl, but I know better than to leave loose ends. She could've blackmailed me down the road and I wasn't having that. Well, I'm glad all of that Russell business is wrapped up. It's time for bed. Oh damn, I cracked my nail. I guess I'll go get my nails done in the morning.

LOVE THIS BOOK AND WANT MORE?

VISIT RYANHODGEBOOKS.COM

MORE BOOKS BY RYAN

The Deception Series:
   *Web of Deception**
   *Wrath of Deception**
   *Will of Deception**
   *Rape by Deception***
   *Woes of Deception**

Historical Science Fiction:
   Reversed World Power

Urban Fiction
   Black Boy Lost, Black Girl Adrift

*Adult romance
**Suspense Thriller. Spin-off of other novels in series

www.ingramcontent.com/pod-product-compliance
Lightning Source LLC
Chambersburg PA
CBHW060112260626
47160CB00005B/1867